DAVE DASHAWAY AND HIS HYDROPLANE

BY

ROY ROCKWOOD

Dave Dashaway And His Hydroplane

CHAPTER I

THE YOUNG AVIATOR

"Telegram, sir."

"Who for?"

"Dave Dashaway."

"I'll take it."

The messenger boy who had just entered the hangar of the great prize monoplane of the aero meet at Columbus, stared wonderingly about him while the man in charge of the place receipted for the telegram.

The lad had never been in so queer a place before. He was a lively, active city boy, but the closest he had ever seen an airship was a distance away and five hundred feet up in the air. Now, with big wonder eyes he stared at the strange appearing machine. His fingers moved restlessly, like a street-urchin surveying an automobile and longing to blow its horn.

The man in charge of the place attracted his attention, too. He had only one arm and limped when he walked. His face was scarred and he looked like a war veteran. The only battles this old warrior had been in, however, were fights with the elements. He was a famous "wind wagon" man who had sustained a terrible fall in an endurance race. It had crippled him for life. Now he followed the various professional meets for a living, and also ran an aviation school for amateurs. His name was John Grimshaw.

The messenger boy took a last look about the place and left. The old man put on a cap, went to the door and rather gruesomely faced the elements.

"A cold drizzling rain and gusty weather generally," he said to himself in a grumbling tone. "I'll face it any time for Dashaway, though. The telegram may be important."

The big aero field looked lonely and gloomy as the man crossed it. Lights showed here and there in the various buildings scattered about the enclosure. The ground was wet and soft. The rain came in chilling dashes. Old Grimshaw breasted the storm, and after half a mile's walk came to a hangar a good deal like the one he had left. There was a light inside.

"Hello, there!" he sang out in his big foghorn voice, thrusting the door open with his foot and getting under the shelter, and shaking the rain from his head and shoulders.

Two boys were the occupants of the place. They had a lamp on the table, upon which was outspread pictures and plans of airships. The older of the two got up from his chair with a pleasant smiling face.

"Why, it's Mr. Grimshaw!" he exclaimed.

"That's who it is," joined in the other boy cheerily. "Say, you're welcome, too. We were looking over some sketches of new machines, and you can tell us lots about them, you know."

"Got to get back to my own quarters," declared Grimshaw. "Some other time about those pictures. Boy brought a telegram to Mr. King's hangar. It's for you, Dashaway."

"For me?" inquired the lad who had first addressed the visitor.

"Yes. Here it is. Mr. King's away, but if you need me for anything let me know."

"I'm always needing you," replied Dave Dashaway. "I don't know what we'd do without you."

The young aviator—for such he was in fact and reality—took the proffered envelope. He tore open its end and read the enclosure rapidly.

"Why," he said, "this is strange."

"Any answer? Need me?" asked Grimshaw, moving towards the door.

"No, thank you," replied Dave in a vague, bothered way that made his companion and chum, Hiram Dobbs, study his face with some perplexity.

"I'd better get back home, then," said the old man. "Fine weather for hydroplanes this, eh?"

Both Dave and Hiram proceeded to the door with the grim old fellow who had so kindly taught them all they knew about aeronautics. When their visitor had departed, Dave went back to the table. He sat down and perused the telegram once more. Then he sat looking fixedly at it, as if he was studying some hard problem. Hiram stood it as long as he could. Then he burst out impetuously:

"What is it, Dave?"

"I'm trying to find out," was the abstracted reply.

"Who is it from?"

"The Interstate Aeroplane Co."

That name meant a good deal to Hiram Dobbs, and a great deal more to Dave Dashaway. It marked the starting point in the aviation career of the latter, and that in its turn had meant a first step up the ladder for his faithful comrade, Hiram.

In the first volume of this series, entitled:
"Dave Dashaway, the Young Aviator; Or, In the Clouds for Fame and Fortune," the career of Dave Dashaway has been told. The father of the young airman had been a noted balloonist, and when he died a mean old skinflint named Silas Warner had been appointed Dave's guardian. Warner had acted the tyrant and hard taskmaster for the youth. A natural love for aeronautics had been born in Dave. He had made an airship model which his guardian had maliciously destroyed. Warner had also appropriated a package dropped accidentally by a famous aviator, named Robert King, from a monoplane.

Dave had found this package, containing money, a watch and a medal greatly prized by Mr. King. Dave resolved that this property should be restored to the airman. He got hold of the lost articles, which his guardian had secreted, and ran away from home.

After various adventures, during which he was robbed of the airman's property, Dave managed to reach the aero meet at Fairfield. He found Robert King and described to him the boy thief. The airman took a fancy to Dave from the nerve and ability he showed in experimenting with a parachute garment, and hired him.

About the same time Hiram Dobbs came along, ambitious to change his farm life for an aviation career, and secured work helping about the grounds. Mr. King sent Dave to Grimshaw for training. The Interstate Aeroplane Co. wanted to exhibit its Baby Racer, a novel biplane. Dave made a successful demonstration, and won the admiration and good will of the company.

In a few weeks time Dave scored a big success and won several trophies. His final exploit was taking the place of an aviator who had fainted away in his monoplane, and winning the race for Mr. King's machine. Dave was now the proud possessor of a pilot's license, and had fairly entered the professional field.

The thief who had stolen Mr. King's property from Dave, a graceless youth named Gregg, was found, and the property recovered. He had also got hold of some papers that belonged to Dave's father. Gregg through these had obtained a trace of a Mr. Dale, a great friend of the dead balloonist. He had made Mr. Dale believe he was the real Dave Dashaway, until he was unmasked.

Another bad boy Dave had run across was named Jerry Dawson. From the start in his career as an airman this youth had been an enemy. Dave had succeeded him in the employ of Mr. King, Jerry having been discharged in disgrace. Jerry tried to "get even," as he called it, by trying to wreck Mr.

King's monoplane, the Aegis. He also betrayed Dave's whereabouts to his guardian. Because Dave was right and Jerry wrong, there plots rebounded on the schemer and did Dave no harm.

Jerry and his father were exposed. They still followed the various meets, however, just as Mr. King and Dave and Hiram did, but they were shunned by all reputable airmen.

After leaving the aero meet at Dayton the proud possessor of a trophy as winner of a one hundred mile dash, Dave now found himself and his friends on the aero, grounds at Columbus. This was a summer resort located on Lake Michigan. A two weeks' programme had been arranged, in which Dave was to give exhibitions for his employers of their new model hydroplane.

Hiram was practicing for a flight in the Baby Racer. The two friends that rainy summer evening were interested in plans for the coming meet and aviation business generally. The arrival of the telegram once more introduces the reader to Dave Dashaway, now popularly known as the young aviator.

The telegram which Grimshaw had brought to Dave was dated at the headquarters of the Interstate Aeroplane Co., some three hundred miles distant. It was addressed to Dave in care of Mr. King, and it was signed by the manager of the company. It read as follows:

"Our sales agent, Timmins, reported from your quarters at Columbus three days ago. Was due at Kewaukee this morning on big contract with County Fair Amusement Co. Wired Northern Hotel there, where we had forwarded all the contracts and papers, and he is not there. Find him at any expense, and get him to Kewaukee before to-morrow morning, or the Star Aero Co. will get the order. Fear some trick. This means ten thousand dollars to us."

Dave read and reread this message, weighing every word in his mind as he did so. Hiram sat watching him in a fever of suspense and anxiety. Finally he exclaimed:

"See here, Dave Dashaway, is that Greek you can't make out, or have you gone to sleep?"

"I was only trying to figure out this telegram," replied Dave thoughtfully. "Here, read it for yourself, and see what you make of it."

The young aviator passed the yellow sheet over to his curious friend. The latter scanned it rapidly. Then, with startling suddenness, his face twitching with excitement, he jumped to his feet.

"What do I make of it?" shouted Hiram. "Just what the telegram says—a trick! It's come all over me in a flash. Why, Dick, I know all about it."

CHAPTER II

The "BABY RACER"

"You know all about it?" repeated Dave Dashaway, looking up in great surprise.

"That's what I do," declared Hiram positively.

"What do you mean?"

"I'll explain."

"I wish you would."

"I'm a blockhead, that's just what I am!" cried Hiram. "I don't know what possessed me that I didn't tell you all about it before."

"See here, Hiram," broke in Dave, "What are you talking about?"

"Why, about Mr. Timmins. You know he here night before last and left us then?"

"Yes, Hiram, to go to Kewaukee."

"Well, he just didn't go to Kewaukee at all."

"That's no news, for this telegram shows that couldn't have done so."

"You see, when Mr. Timmins got telling us about the big sale he was going to make at Kewaukee," continued Hiram, "and how the Star Aero people were bidders for the same contract, you warned him against the Dawsons, and the people they are working for!"

"I know I did. That was because the Dawsons are stunting for the

Star people."

"Exactly. Then when I caught Jerry Dawson and Brooks, that precious chum of his, sneaking around the Aegis hangar, I made up my mind that they were up to no good. I know what they were snooping around for, now."

"What was it?"

"To pick up what information they could about Mr. Timmins' plans, so, when Mr. Timmins went away, I was awful glad. I felt pleased, for Mr. King told as you know that he was a free and easy fellow, friendly to everybody, and sometimes drank more than he ought to."

"Yes, I know that, Hiram."

"Well, last night I went to town to get some supplies for Mr. Grimshaw. There's a tavern at the cross roads, and some men were in there. I saw them through an open window. There were six of them. Brooks was there, and Jerry and his father, and three more of the crowd. They were playing cards and making a great deal of noise. Just as I looked in some one pulled down the shade. I caught a sight of the other man, though. Right off, even at the distance I was, it struck me he looked like Mr. Timmins. Then I remembered that Mr. Timmins had certainly gone to Kewaukee the night before, so I put it off my mind. Now, I see the whole trick."

"What is that?"

"The crowd kept Mr. Timmins here, delaying and entertaining him.

Maybe later some of them led him still further away from Columbus.

Their man is probably on the spot at Kewaukee now, ready to get that

big contract for show biplanes."

Dave had been anxiously walking up and down the floor while Hiram was talking. Now he took his cap off a peg and picked up an umbrella.

"You wait here till I come back, Hiram," he said.

"Where are you going, Dave?"

"Down to the Aegis hangar. This telegram disturbs me very much. I have no idea where Mr. Timmins can be, and something must certainly be done about this contract."

"That's so, Dave," agreed Hiram. "It isn't exactly our business, but it would be a big feather in your cap to help out the people who are hiring you."

"That's what I want to do, if I can," replied Dave, as he left the place.

The youth went straight to the Aegis hangar, where he found Grimshaw tinkering over a broken airplane wing. Mr. King had a desk in one corner of what he called his office room.

Dave was free to use this at all times. He opened it now, and for ten minutes was busy with some railroad time tables he found there. Then he consulted an aero guide map.

Grimshaw watched him from under his shaggy eyebrows, but said nothing until Dave got up from the desk, buttoned his coat and prepared to face the storm again.

"What's the trouble, Dashaway?" he asked.

"Why, Mr. Grimshaw?" inquired Dave, wishing to evade direct questioning.

"You seem bothered about something, I see."

"Well, as a matter of fact, I am," confessed Dave.

"What is it?"

"I'm trying to find a way to get to Kewaukee," explained Dave. "Something has come up that makes me think I ought to be there in the interests of my employers early to-morrow morning. I am figuring out how I can make it."

"See here, Dashaway," spoke the old airman in a grim, impressive way, "don't you do anything reckless."

"I won't," answered Dave. "You know you once said I was all business. Well, I'll always try to do my duty without any unnecessary risks."

Dave laughed carelessly and got away from the hangar. A daring idea had come into his mind. Perhaps Grimshaw suspected it, and Dave was afraid he might. The lad knew that the eccentric old fellow liked him, and would try to dissuade him from any exploit of unusual peril.

"I'll do it, I'll have to do it or let the company lose out," breathed Dave, as once outside he broke into a run across the aviation field.

Dave found Hiram winding the alarm clock as he re-entered the half shed, half canvas house where the Baby Racer was stored. Although they got their meals at Mr. King's headquarters, the boys had two light cots and slept near to the machine which Dave had been exhibiting.

Dave glanced at the clock, and Hiram noticing the look, said:

"Eleven thirty, Dave. I've set the alarm clock for five thirty. You know that new hydroplane will probably come in on an early freight. What's the programme?"

"Well, Hiram," responded Dave, throwing off his coat and hat, "I'm going to dress up for a ride."

"Eh?" ejaculated Hiram, staring hard at the set resolute face of his comrade.

"Yes, I've got to get to Kewaukee."

"Oh, you mean going by train?"

"No. Last one left an hour ago. Next one nine o clock to-morrow morning."

"Automobile, then?"

"On the country mud roads we've been having for the last week?"

"That's so. Then—"

"It's the airship route or nothing, Hiram," said Dave. "I'm going in the biplane."

"The Baby Racer?"

"Yes."

"On such a night as this! Why, Dave," began Hiram, almost in alarm.

"Don't say a word," interrupted Dave with a preemptory wave of his hand. "I've made up my mind, and that ends it."

"It usually does," said Hiram. "If you're bound to do it, though, Dave—"

"I certainly am."

"Ask Mr. Grimshaw's advice, first."

"Not for worlds."

"Why not?"

"I think he would try to stop me. See here, Hiram, I've thought it all over. I know it's a hard, rough night, but I also know what the Baby Racer can do."

"It's a pretty bad night to do any fooling in the air," remarked Hiram.

"There won't be much fooling about it, Hiram. I know the chances and, I shan't look for any fun. It is a bad night, I know, but the wind is right, and I can head straight into it in reaching Kewaukee."

"How far away is Kewaukee, Dave?"

"Ninety-five miles."

Dave, while he talked, had been putting on his regular aviator's suit. As he finished up with a helmet, he noticed Hiram changing his coat for a sweater.

"What are you up to, Hiram," he inquired quickly.

"Getting ready, of course."

"Getting ready for what?"

"The trip to Kewaukee."

"Oh, you think you're going?"

"If you are," retorted Hiram, "I know I am. Now, see here, Dave," continued Hiram, waving a silencing finger as Dave was about to speak, "I know I'm not an aviator like you, and never will be. All the same, I am some good in an airship, if it's only to act as ballast. The other day when I was up with you in the Racer, you. said I shifted the elevator just in time to save a smash up. In a storm like the one to-night, you my need me worse than ever. Anyhow, Dave Dashaway, I won't let you go alone."

The young airman looked at his loyal, earnest friend with pleasure and pride. Hiram was only a crude country boy. He had, however, shown diamond in the rough, and Dave appreciated the fact.

Hiram had made several ground runs in an aeroplane. He had gone up in the Baby Racer twice with Dave, and had proven himself a model passenger. As he had just hinted, too, he had been familiar enough with the mechanism of the biplane to operate some of its auxiliary machinery so as to avert an accident.

"You are the best company in the world, Hiram," said Dave, "but I wouldn't feel right in letting you take the risk of a hazardous run."

"Dave, I won't let you go alone," persisted Hiram.

Dave said nothing in reply. He went outside, and Hiram followed him. They unlocked the door of the shed adjoining where the Baby Racer was housed, and lit two lanterns.

"Get a couple of the nearest field men, Hiram," directed Dave, "and

I will have everything in order by the time you get back."

There was not much for Dave to do. Only the noon of that day they had got the little biplane ready for a cross country spurt. Then the rain came on, and they decided to defer the dash till the weather was more propitious. Dave was looking over the machinery, when a gruff hail startled him.

"Hello!" challenged old Grimshaw, appearing at the open doorway of the hangar. "What you up to, Dashaway?"

Dave flushed guiltily. He was dreadfully embarrassed to be "caught in the act" as it were, by his great friend, the old airman.

"Why—you see, Mr. Grimshaw—" stammered Dave.

"Yes, of course I see," retorted the old man firmly. "You're going to start out a night like this."

"I've got to, Mr. Grimshaw," declared Dave desperately.

"Business, eh?"

"Of the most important kind."

"What is it?"

It was in order for Dave to explain details, and did so briefly.

"H'm," commented Grimshaw, when his pupil concluded his explanation.

"And so you thought you'd steal away without letting me know it?"

"Oh, now, Mr. Grimshaw!" Dave hastened to say—"that was not the spirit of the thing at all."

"Go ahead, Dashaway."

"Well, then, I think so very much of you I didn't want it to worry you."

"Roll her out," was all that Grimshaw would say, placing his one hand on the tail of the biplane. "Hold on for a minute. Gasoline supply?"

"Twenty-five gallons."

"That will do. Lubricating oil-all right. Now then, lad, hit that head wind every time, and you'll make it, sure."

CHAPTER III

A WILD NIGHT RIDE

"Go!"

It was less than half an hour after the appearance of Grimshaw on the scene that the Baby Racer was all ready for its stormy night's flight.

The old aviator had fussed and poked about the dainty little biplane, as if it was some valued friend he was sending out into the world to try its fortune. Every once in a while he had growled out some brief advice to Dave in his characteristic way.

Then he directed and helped, while two field men started the machine on its forward run.

"Look out for telegraph poles, and watch your fuel tank," was

Grimshaw's final injunction.

Dave knew the Baby Racer just as an engineer understands his locomotive. Daylight or dirk, once aloft the young aviator did not doubt his own powers. The moment the Racer left the ground, however, with a switch of her flapping tail, Dave knew that he was to have no easy fair-weather cruise.

"Slow it is," the watchful, excited Hiram heard him say, working the wheel as cautiously as an automobilist rounding a sharp curve.

Dave saw that everything depended on getting a start and reaching a higher level. He kept the angle of ascent small, for the maximum power of the engine could not be reached in a moment. The starting speed naturally let down with the machine ascending an inclined plane.

"It's slow enough, that's sure," remarked Hiram. "It's the wind, isn't it, Dave?"

"We don't want to slide back in the air or be blown over backwards," replied Dave, eye, ear, and nerve on the keenest alert.

The wind resistance caused a growing speed reduction. The sensitiveness of the elevating rudder warned Dave that he must maintain a perfect balance until they could strike a steady path of flight. Hiram's rapt gaze followed every skillful maneuver of the master hand at that wheel.

"Good for you!" he chirped, as Dave worked the ailerons to counteract the leaning of the machine. A swing of the rudder had caused the biplane to bank, but quick as a flash Dave righted it by getting the warping control on the opposite tack, avoiding a bad spill.

The machine was tail heavy as Dave directed a forward plunge, coasting slightly. He had, however, pretty good control of the center of gravity.

It was now only a question of fighting the stiff breeze that prevailed, and keeping an even balance.

Hiram's eyes sparkled as the Racer volplaned, caught the head wind at just the right angle, and struck a course due northwest like a sail boat under perfect control.

The engine was near the operator's seat, and on the post just under the wheel were the spark and throttle levers on the fuselage beam. The steering wheel was a solid piece of wood about eight inches in diameter with two holes cut into it to fit the hands.

The passenger's seat now occupied by Hiram was in the center line of the machine, so that, filled or vacant, the lateral balance was not affected.

Hiram knew all about the monoplane dummy or the aerocycle with treadle power for practice work which he had operated under old Grimshaw's direction. As to the practical running of a biplane aloft, however, that was something for him to learn. He was keenly alive to every maneuver that Dave executed, and he stored in his mind every new point he noticed as the Racer seemed fairly started on its way.

"Keep me posted, Dave," spoke the willing Hiram. "If anything happens I want to know what you expect me to do."

"I don't intend to have anything happen if I can help it, Hiram," replied Dave. "This is a famous start."

"It's not half as bad as I thought it would be," said Hiram.

The rain had changed into a fine mist, but the breeze continued choppy and strong at times. Dave had gone over the course with Mr. King in The Aegis twice in the daytime, and had an accurate idea of the route. However, he had landmarks to follow. What guided Dave were the lights of the various towns on the route to Kewaukee and railway signals. These were dimly outlined by a glow only at times, but Dave as he progressed felt that he was keeping fairly close to his outlined programme.

Hiram chuckled and warbled, as he knew from Dave's manner and the way the Baby Racer acted that his friend had it under full control. Our hero attempted no fancy flying nor spurts of swiftness. Up to the end of the first hour the flight had proven far less difficult than he had anticipated.

"There's Medbury," said Dave at length, inclining his head towards a cluster of electric lights below and somewhat beyond them. "That means one-third of our journey covered."

"It's great what you and the Baby Racer can do, Dave," cried the admiring and enthusiastic country boy. "We're going to make it, aren't we?"

"If the wind doesn't change and we meet with no mishaps," answered Dave.

A stretch of steady sailing was an excuse for Hiram to share a brief lunch of ham sandwiches with Dave. The thoughtful Grimshaw had provided these at the last moment of the departure of the biplane.

By the watch Mr. King had given him on the occasion of winning a race for the Aegis, Dave found that it was a little after two o'clock when the Racer passed a town named Creston.

"It's only twenty miles farther, Hiram," announced the young aviator with satisfaction.

"And plenty of juice in the tank left to go on," added Hiram. "This is a trip to talk about, eh, Dave?"

Dave nodded and smiled. He suddenly gave renewed attention to wheel and levers.

"Anything wrong?" inquired Hiram, noticing the movement.

"The wind is shifting slightly," was the reply.

Dave felt of the breeze cautiously after that, keeping his cheek well to windward. It required constant watchfulness and maneuvering for the next fifteen miles to keep the control permanent. Dave was glad when a dim glow of radiance told that they had nearly reached the end of their journey.

Dave "ducked," as the phrase goes, as a swoop from a new quarter sent the machine banking.

He managed the dilemma by circling. There was only five more miles to cover. Dave went up searching for a steadier air current, found it, maintained a steady flight for over a quarter of an hour, and slowed down slightly as they came directly over Kewaukee.

"Going to land?" inquired Hiram, attentively attracted by all these skillful maneuvers.

"Yes," replied Dave. "The question is, though, to find just the right place."

Dave tried to figure out the contour of the landscape beneath them. He passed over high buildings, skirted what seemed like a factory district, and began to volplane.

"Going to drop?" queried Hiram.

"I think so," responded Dave. "According to those electric lights there is a park or some other large vacant space we can strike on this angle."

"The mischief!" exclaimed Hiram abruptly as the Racer struck a lower air current a strong blast of wind made it shake and reel. Then there was a creak, a sway and a snap.

"Something broke!" shouted Hiram in excitement.

"Yes," answered Dave rapidly. "It's one of the right outermost struts between the supporting planes."

"The one that snapped the other day," suggested Hiram.

"Likely. Grimshaw fixed it with glue and bracing, and fitting iron rings about it. The vibration of the motor and the straining have pulled the nail heads through the holes in the rings."

"Can you hold out?"

Dave did not reply. He felt new vibrations, and knew that the strain of warping the wings at the tips had caused more than one of the struts to collapse.

The young aviator realized that it would be a hard drop unless he did something quickly and effectively. There was no time to think. Counterbalance was everything.

Dave tried to restore the disturbed balance of the machine by bringing the left wing under the control. Then he forced the twisting on the right side.

The young aviator held his breath, while his excited companion stared ahead and down, transfixed. They were going at a rapid rate, and every moment the Baby Racer threatened to turn turtle and spill them out.

Dave succeeded in temporarily checking the tendency to tip. All aerial support was gone. He kept the rudder at counterbalance, threw off the power, and wondered what they were headed into.

The next moment the Baby Racer crashed to the ground.

CHAPTER IV

A BUSINESS BOY

"We've landed!" shouted Hiram in a jolty tone, plunging forward in his seat in the biplane.

"Yes, but where?" Dave asked quickly.

"That's so. Whew! What have we drifted into?"

The Baby Racer had struck a mass soft and yielding. It drove through some substance rather than ran on its wheels. There was a dive and a joggle. Then the machine came to a halt—submerged.

Whatever had received it now came up about the puzzled young aviators as might a snowdrift or it heap of hay. Dave dashed a filmy, flake-like substance resembling sawdust from eyes, ears and mouth. Hiram tried to disentangle himself from strips and curls of some light, fluffy substance. Then he cried out:

"Dave, it's shavings!"

"You don't say so."

"Yes, it is—a great heap of shavings, a big mountain of them."

"Lucky for us. If we had hit the bare ground I fear we would have had a smash up."

Gradually and cautiously the two young aviators made their way out of the seats of the machine. They got past the wings. A circle of electric street lamps surrounded them on four sides. Their radiance, dim and distant, seemed to indicate that they were in the center of a factory yard covering several acres.

A little way off they could discern the outlines of high piles of lumber and beyond these several buildings. The biplane lay partly on its side, sunk deep in a heap of long, broad shavings. The mass must have been fully a hundred feet in extent and fifteen to twenty feet high. They reached its side and slid down the slant to the ground.

"Well!" ejaculated Dave.

"Yes, and what?" inquired Hiram, brushing the loose bits of shavings from his soaked tarpaulin coat.

"Business—strictly and quick," replied Dave promptly.

"And leave the Racer where she is?"

"Can you find a better place, Hiram?"

"Well, no, but—"

A man flashing a dark lantern and armed with a heavy cane came upon them around the corner of the buildings. The boys paused. The man, evidently the watchman of the place, challenged them, moving his lantern from face to face.

"Who are you?" he demanded sternly.

"Aviators," replied Dave.

"What's that?"

"We just arrived in an airship."

"No nonsense. How did you get in here?"

"Mister," spoke out Hiram, "we just landed in the biplane, the Baby Racer. If you don't believe me, come to the shavings pile yonder and we'll show you the machine, and thank you for having it there, for if you hadn't I guess we'd have needed an ambulance."

The watchman looked incredulous. He followed Dave and Hiram, however, as they led the way back to the heap of shavings. One wing of the biplane stuck up in the air and he made it out.

"This is queer," he observed. "You say it's an airship?"

"Yes, sir," nodded Hiram.

"We had to make a hurried night journey from Columbus," explained

Dave. "There were no trains, and we came with the biplane."

"Well, well, well," commented the watchman. He had heard of

Columbus and the aero meet there, and began to understand matters.

"You see," spoke Hiram, "we can't land everywhere, or we'd have to settle some damage suits."

"I will be glad to pay you for letting us leave the machine here till after daylight, and watch it to see no harm comes to it," proposed Dave.

"Why, we'll do that," assented the watchman. "You look like two decent young fellows, and I'm sure the company won't object to letting your airship stay up there for a few hours."

"We will be back to see about it in a few hours," promised Dave.

The watchman led the boys to the big gate of the factory yard and let them out. The rain had ceased and the wind was not blowing so hard as before.

"What now, Dave?" inquired Hiram, as they found themselves in the deserted street.

"The Northern Hotel."

"Oh, going to try and fix things before daylight?"

"We can't afford to lose a minute," declared Dave. "There's a policeman. I want to ask him a question."

They hurried to a corner where a policeman had halted under the street lamp. Dave inquired the location of the Northern Hotel. Then the boys proceeded again on their way, and reached the place in about half an hour.

The night clerk and others were on duty. Dave approached the desk and addressed the clerk.

"Is a Mr. Timmins stopping here?" he asked.

"Why, no," replied the clerk, looking Dave and Hiram over curiously, their somewhat queer garb attracting his attention.

"Do you know him, may I inquire?"

"Oh, yes, Mr. Timmins has been here several times. We are holding some mail for him, and expected him several days ago."

"Do you know the company he represents?"

"Airships, isn't it?" propounded the clerk.

"That's right. The Interstate Aeroplane Company."

"Yes, I remember now," added the clerk.

"I am also connected with that company," explained Dave.

The clerk stared vaguely, as if he did not quite understand the situation.

"Yes," eagerly broke in the irrepressible Hiram, as if he was introducing some big magnate, "he's Dave Dashaway, and he's beat the field with the Interstate Baby Racer."

"Oh, Dashaway, eh?" said the clerk, with a pleasant smile. "I've heard of you and read about you."

"I am glad of that," responded Dave, "because it may help you identify me with the Inter-state people. As an employee of theirs and a friend of Mr. Timmins, I will have to be confidential with you."

"That's all right—we are used to confidences in this business," said the hotel clerk.

Dave reflected deeply for a moment. He had a definite plan in view.

He realized that he must confide to a degree in the hotel clerk.

"The gist of the matter," said Dave, "is that Mr. Timmins has missed connections. He should have been here two days ago. Here is a telegram I received from the Interstate people."

The clerk read the telegram. He nodded his head and smiled, which the observant Dave took to mean that he was friendly towards Mr. Timmins, but knew of some of his business-lapses in the past.

"What do you want me to do?" asked the clerk.

"You notice that the Interstate people refer in that telegram to some papers sent to the hotel here for Mr. Timmins."

"I noticed that," assented the clerk. "I shouldn't wonder if this is the package."

As he spoke the clerk reached over to the letter case near his desk

and took up a large manila envelope. It was addressed to Mr.

Timmins, and bore in one corner the printed name and address of the

Interstate Aeroplane Co.

"That is the letter, I feel sure," said Dave.

"I have no doubt of it," agreed the clerk.

"Do you suppose it would help you out any to have me give it to you?"

"Why, will you?" questioned Dave eagerly. "I was going to ask you to do so."

"I think I understand the situation now," said the clerk, "and I can see how your getting the letter may help your people out of a tangle. It's taking some responsibility on my part, for the letter is of course the property of Mr. Timmins. I'm going to take the risk, though, and I think Mr. Timmins will say it's all right when he comes along."

"I know he will," declared Dave. "You see, I hope to carry through a contract he has neglected."

Dave took the bulky letter and opened its envelope. He glanced hastily but intelligently over its contents. They were just what he imagined they would be, contracts for eight biplanes ready to sign, and details and plans as to the machines.

"Have you a Kewaukee directory here?" he asked.

The clerk pushed a bulky volume across the marble slab of the counter, with the words:

"Anybody special you are looking up?"

"Why, yes," replied Dave, "the County Fair Amusement Co."

"Oh, you mean Col. Lyon's proposition," observed the clerk at once.

"He runs county fair attractions all over the country."

"It must be the same," said Dave.

"I know Col. Lyon very well," proceeded the clerk. "He comes in here very often."

"Where is his office?" inquired Dave.

"I don't think he has any regular office," responded the clerk.

"Two or three times a week he calls for mail at the Central

Amusement Exchange. He travels a good deal—has side attractions with most of the big shows."

"But he lives in Kewaukee?"

"Not exactly. He has a very fine place called Fernwood, out on the North Boulevard."

Dave thought things over for a minute or two. Then he asked:

"How can I reach Fernwood?"

"You don't mean before daylight?"

"Why, yes," responded Dave, "the sooner the better."

"I think any of the taxi men out at the curb know the location," said the clerk.

"Thank you," replied Dave, "and for all your great kindness about that letter."

He and Hiram went out to the street. There were three or four taxicabs lined up at the curb, their drivers napping in the seats. Dave approached one of them.

"Do you know where Fernwood is?" he inquired of the chauffeur.

"You mean Col. Lyon's place?"

"Yes."

"Was there only last night. I took the Colonel home."

"Then he's there," spoke Dave to Hiram. "All right, take us to Fernwood."

"You won't find anybody stirring at this hour of the morning," suggested the chauffeur.

"Then we'll Wait till the Colonel gets up," said Dave.

In less than half an hour the auto came to a halt before one of a score or more of fine houses lining the most exclusive section of the country boulevard.

Dave got out of the machine and Hiram followed him. They passed through the gates of a large garden. In its center was a mansion with wide porches. No light showed anywhere about the place.

"You're not going to wake anybody up at this outlandish hour?" asked Hiram.

"Well, perhaps not," answered Dave.

"Why didn't you wait and see this Col. Lyon in the city at his office?"

"Because there is no certainty that he will be at his office today. Then, too, that Star fellow may be on hand there to grab the contract. I want to head him off."

By this time they had reached the steps of the front porch.

"See here, Hiram," observed Dave, lowering his voice, "we'll sit down here for a spell. It's about five o'clock, and by six someone will be stirring about."

"Say," said Hiram, staring across the shadowed porch, "the front door there is open."

"Why, so it is," replied Dave, peering towards it.

"That's strange, isn't it?"

"Oh, no—neglected, or left open for ventilation."

Both boys relapsed into silence. Hiram rested his face on his hands and his knees, inclined to doze.

Dave was framing up in his mind how he would approach Col. Lyon. He was deeply immersed in thought, when a sound behind him caused him to start and look behind him.

Somebody with a great bundle done up in a sheet had just passed through the open doorway out upon the porch.

The bundle was so big that its bearer had both hands clasped about it, and its top came above his eyes.

Before Dave could speak a warning, the man carrying the package crossed the porch and stumbled against Hiram, whom he did not see.

"Thunder! what's this?" shouted Hiram, knocked from his position and rolling down the steps.

The man with the bundle echoed the try with one of alarm, as he missed his footing and plunged forward.

"The mischief!" exclaimed Dave, starting at the bundle over which the man tumbled, bursting it open.

There was an immense clatter. Even in the imperfect light of the early morning, the young aviator made out a great heap of clothing, silverware and jewelry, rattling down the steps of the porch.

CHAPTER V

A TEN THOUSAND DOLLAR ORDER

"What's happened?" cried Hiram, rolling over and over on the gravel walk to which he had tumbled.

"Stop that man!" shouted Dave.

In a flash the young aviator took in the meaning of the situation. The fugitive, for such he now was, made a quick move the instant he gained his feet. Not waiting to see who had obstructed his progress, and probably deciding that it was the police, he bounded in among some bushes.

Dave, running after him, made out his form dimly, swiftly scaling a rear brick wall.

"Why, what is all this?" demanded Hiram, staring at the litter on the steps.

"That man was a thief," explained Dave.

"It looks that way, doesn't it? Hello!"

Both boys stepped back and stared upwards. Over the porch was a second railed-in veranda. A night-robed figure had crossed it from some bed chamber fronting upon it.

"Hey, you down there! What's all this racket?" challenged this newcomer on the scene.

"Are you Colonel Lyon?" inquired Dave.

"That's me."

"Then you had better come down and see what's going on."

"Why so?"

"Your house has been burglarized."

"Gracious I you don't say so. Where is the thief?"

"He has escaped."

"Hm. Down in a minute," mumbled the man, retiring from view.

It was several minutes before the owner of the mansion put in a second appearance. He came cautiously out on the porch, clutching a great heavy cane. He looked the boys over suspiciously.

"I don't understand this," he began.

"Neither did we, Mister," returned Hiram, "till the thief came bolting out through that front door. He fell all over me and dropped his bundle. There's what was in it."

Hiram pointed to the scattered plunder. For the first time the colonel caught sight of the scattered stuff. He gasped, and stared, and fidgeted. Then he hastened back across the porch and into the vestibule.

Clang! clang! Clang! rang out a great alarm gong, and almost immediately two men servants of the place came rushing out half-dressed upon the porch.

In a very much excited way the colonel incoherently told of the burglary. He ordered the men to gather up the scattered plunder. Then he turned his attention to Dave and Hiram.

"Now, tell me about the whole thing," he spoke.

"There isn't much to tell, Colonel Lyon," replied Dave. "We were sitting here waiting—"

"Waiting?" repeated the showman sharply.

"Yes, sir."

"What for?"

"To see you."

"Eh?" projected the Colonel, with a stare.

"That's right, Mister," declared Hiram. "You see, it's pretty early, and we didn't want to wake you up."

"Yes, but what brought you here so early?"

"Business," answered Dave.

"Business—with me?"

"Yes, sir. We came in an automobile from the city, so as to be sure to find you early enough. We had just settled down here to wait and rest, when that burglar came out."

"Why, then, you've saved my losing all that valuable stuff!" exclaimed the showman. "I should say so," added the speaker with force, as he moved over and glanced at the heaps his servants were massing together, upon the lower step. "Watches, rings, silverware, my fur winter coat, and hello—my whole collection of rare coins! Hump! the man must have had the run of the house for hours. Here, you two, come inside. You've done me a big service."

Hiram chuckled, nudging Dave in a knowing way.

"What luck!" he whispered. "Dave, you're all right now."

The owner of the place led his young guests through the vestibule into a hallway, and pointed to a large reception room.

"You wait till I get dressed," he directed. "Sit down, and make yourself comfortable."

As he spoke the showman turned on a perfect blaze of electric light. Dave and Hiram took off their helmets, and made themselves look as little like stormy night aviators as was possible under the circumstances.

It was nearly ten minutes before their host reappeared. He was fully dressed now, and presented the appearance of a keen, active business man.

"Think there's any use trying to catch that burglar?" was his first question.

"I don't think so at all," replied Dave.

"All right, then. Carry that truck into the library," the showman ordered his two men, who had gathered it up in a rug taken from the vestibule. "You'll take turns guarding the house, nights after this. Now then, young men, who are you?"

The showman put the question as he plumped down in an armchair besides his two guests.

"We're airship boys," explained Hiram hastily, but proudly.

"Oh!" commented Colonel Lyon slowly, looking the pair over from head to foot.

"That is, Dave is an airman," corrected Hiram. "He's Dave

Dashaway."

"Why, I've heard of you. At the Dayton meet, weren't you?

Honorable mention, or was it a prize?"

"Both," shot out Hiram promptly.

"That's very good," said the colonel. "I'm pretty well up in the aero field myself. I run that line at county fairs."

"Yes, sir, I know that," said Dave, "and that is why I came to see you."

"That's so—you said it was business, but I must say you are early birds," smiled the showman.

"We had to be," again spoke Hiram.

"How was that?"

"Why," said Dave, "I thought it was very necessary that I should see you first thing this morning. I acted on a wire from my employers, the Interstate Aeroplane Co."

"Your employers?" repeated the colonel, a fresh token of interest in his eyes.

"Yes, sir, I have been exhibiting their Baby Racer at the meets."

"Ah, I understand now."

"I am going to take up hydroplane work at Columbus, now. Last night late I received a telegram from the Interstate people. It led to getting to Kewaukee and seeing you. There were no trains."

"Roads too bad for an automobile," put in Hiram.

"And we came in the Baby Racer," concluded Dave.

"What's that?" exclaimed the showman.

"You came all the way from Columbus in a biplane?"

"Yes, sir," nodded Dave.

"A night like last night—"

"We had to, you see," observed Hiram.

"H'm," observed the colonel, with decided admiration in his manner, "that was a big thing to do. Where is your machine?"

"We landed on a heap of shavings in a city factory yard," explained

Dave. "We left the machine in charge of the watchman."

"And automobiled it out here? Why, say, I had some dealings with your company."

"I know you did," said Dave.

"I wrote to them for specifications and figures on light biplanes.

They sent outlines that pleased me very much, and I told them so.

Their man made an appointment to be at my city office to close up

matters day before yesterday. He never showed up."

"I know that," said Dave.

"What was the trouble?"

"I will explain that to you."

"You see, the Star man was here yesterday. He made a pretty fair showing, but I was rather struck on your goods."

"Everybody is that knows them," spoke Hiram.

"Well, I was to let the man know this morning at my city office my decision. You are on deck. All right, what have you got to say?"

"Why, just this," replied Dave: "I'm not much of a business man, of course, but I hurried on to see you because I believe a trick has been played on our people."

"Who by?"

"The Star crowd."

"Oh!"

"In some way they have sidetracked our agent. I have with me," continued Dave, "the detailed plans and figures on your order, which had been forwarded from the factory to the Northern Hotel, at Kewaukee."

"All right, show them up," directed the colonel briskly.

Dave did so. Hiram sat regarding his friend, with undisguised admiration, as for one half, hour Dave went over papers, explaining the merits of the Interstate biplane with all the clearness and ability of a born salesman.

"You'll do," pronounced the showman with an expansive smile, as

Dave concluded. "That's the contract, is it?"

"Yes, sir," and Dave handed the showman the paper in question.

"All right, I'll just go to the library and sign it."

"Dave," whispered Hiram in a triumphant chuckle, as Colonel Lyon left the room. "Great!"

Dave returned a pleased smile. He suppressed partly the great satisfaction he felt.

"You see," remarked the showman, returning in a few minutes and handing the signed contract to Dave, "I favored your machines from the start. It must be a good machine, to make ninety miles on a night like last night. Now then, young gentlemen, I've ordered an early breakfast, and I want you to join me at the meal."

There was no gainsaying the hearty, imperious old fellow. The boys felt first class as they finished a repast that sent them on their way complacent and delighted.

"The company will acknowledge the contract, Colonel Lyon," said

Dave, as they left the porch, "and attend to other details."

"I don't suppose, Dashaway," answered the showman, "that you're open for such a week stunt as exhibiting at some of my county fairs?"

"I am under contract with the Interstate people," replied Dave. "If I get out of a job, Colonel Lyon, I shall be glad to have you consider me."

"I fancy I will," declared the showman with enthusiasm. "I'll make you a liberal offer, too. You've saved the carting away of all that stuff the burglar gathered. It make it up to you some way."

Dave waved the contract in reply.

"I couldn't have a better feather in my cap than this," he cried gaily. "Many, many, thanks, Colonel Lyon."

"And you'll find the Interstate biplane just the best in the world," added Hiram.

"We've kept that chauffeur waiting a long time," observed Dave, as they came out upon the boulevard.

"Oh, he's used to that," suggested Hiram.

"I'll give him something extra for his patience," said Dave.

"Yes, the Interstate people can well afford it," commented Hiram.

"Think of it: a ten thousand dollar order! Hurrah!"

CHAPTER VI

ABOARD THE HYDROPLANE

"Dashaway, you're a wonder."

"Thank you, sir."

"And I'm proud of you," added Mr. Robert King, the winner of the monoplane endurance prize, and the man who had practically adopted Dave into the aviation field.

"I've got something to say as to the matter of pride," spoke up old

Grimshaw. "A lad who can make the run Dashaway did with the Baby

Racer, is a boy to holler about."

"If there's anything to be proud about," added Dave, "it's the right good friends I've made."

"My friends, too," put in the impetuous Hiram. "I'm getting along famously. Why, I only tipped out of the dummy airship once yesterday."

All hands were in fine high spirits. It was several days after the wild night race Dave and Hiram had made to Kewaukee. Now the entire party were on their way to the borders of the lake, where the new hydroplane made by the Interstate Aviation Company was ready for a trial trip. Grimshaw knew little of hydroplanes, and the Interstate people had sent an expert demonstrator to the spot to teach their young exhibitor the ropes. Dave had been constantly under this man's tuition.

It was far more easy, he had learned, to acquire a thorough knowledge, of how to run a hydroplane than to operate a monoplane. It was simpler, and besides that his experience with an airship helped wonderfully.

Dave was winning golden opinions from his employers. The way in which he had dosed the Kewaukee contract had pleased them immensely. There was another end to the Kewaukee episode that had brought heaps of satisfaction to all of them, especially to Hiram Dobbs.

The Baby Racer had been quickly repaired at Kewaukee, and had made a speedy return trip to Columbus. Somehow the story of how the Interstate people had outwitted the plots of the Star crowd had gotten noised around the meet. Then a class journal devoted to aeronautics printed the story.

"Well," Hiram had come to Mr. King's hangar that morning to say, "the Dawson crowd are simply squelched. I met Jerry Dawson and his father. You ought to see the looks they gave me when I just grinned at them, and said 'Contract!' It was like a fellow saying 'Baa!' to sheep. Why, those fellows just sneaked away. We've beaten them at every angle, Dave, and I reckon they'll give up their meanness now, and quickly fade away."

"It would be a good thing for honest aeronautics if they would," growled old Grimshaw.

"We'll hasten them with a little help, if they try any more tricks," announced Mr. King.

The hydroplane had been run into a boat house after the practice of the day previous, and was all ready for use. It was equipped to carry two or more passengers, and was driven by a fifty horse power motor. It had two propellers, and these were controlled by chain transmission.

Old Grimshaw had not much use for hydroplanes, he had told Dave. His hobby was air machines. However, because his favorite pupil was going to run the machine, he allowed Dave to explain about the hydroplane, and was quite interested.

The machine had a bulkhead fore and aft, with an upward slope in front and a downward slope to the rear.

"It's safe, comfortable, and quick to rise to control," declared

Dave. "See, Mr. Grimshaw, there's a new wrinkle."

Dave touched a little device attached to the flywheel. The latter was made with teeth to fit into another gear, operated from a shaft.

"What do you call that, now?" asked the old airman.

"A self starter. You see, the shaft runs forward alongside the pilot's seat. Here's the handle of it, right at the end of the shaft."

"Looks all right," admitted Grimshaw grudgingly. "Give me the air, though, every time. If you want to be a sailor, why don't you enlist the navy?"

"How about an air and water combination, Grimshaw?" called Mr. King.

"Well, that is a little better," replied Grimshaw.

"I'm dying to see that new aero-hydroplane Dave's people are getting out," remarked the ardent Hiram.

"They wrote me it would be completed this week," said Dave.

"And you are going to run it, Dave?"

"I think so, I hope so. They claim great things for it."

"Well, give your hydroplane a spin, Dashaway," suggested Mr. King. "I want to see how she works, and must get back to the hangars on business."

The Reliance, the new hydroplane of the Interstate people, was twenty feet long and had a fuel gauge and a bilge pump.

Dave got into his seat, and Hiram sat directly beside him. A touch put the machinery in motion.

"There's a puffy eighteen mile wind, Dashaway," cried out Mr. King.

"Yes, I wouldn't venture too far from shore," advised Grimshaw, a trifle anxiously.

The water was quite rough where the flight started. The machine acted all right, however. A crowd had gathered on the beach, and there was some encouraging cheering as the power boat gained good headway.

"Whew I what have you invited me to, Dave—bath?" puffed Hiram.

Dave had neglected to put in place the rubber cover, so that during the preliminary run along the water the waves drenched both of the boys.

Dave stopped the motor and started drifting, at a sudden current or breeze sent the tail before the wind. The rear of the hydroplane was forced under water.

"Look out!" ordered Dave sharply.

"I see—we're in for an upset," spoke Hiram quickly.

The hydroplane was forced over backwards, the tail striking a sand bar.

Dave and Hiram were both ready for the tip. They escaped with only wetting their feet, for they climbed upon the bottom of the upper surface as the hydro capsized.

The hydroplanes prevented the machine from sinking. Almost at once a boat put out from shore. Once back at the boat house, the damage shown was a slight fracture to the main girder and some of the ribs at the trailing edge, and two broken tail spars. Dave sent Hiram at once to the practice grounds to arrange about the repairs.

"It's no weather for a trial, Dashaway," said Mr. King, "I think I would postpone the trial trip until tomorrow, if I were you."

Dave did not commit himself. He stayed about the boat house after the airman and Grimshaw had gone away, watching every move of the repair man.

"She's staunch and sound as she was at the beginning," the latter declared, when he had completed his work.

"Yes, I think that is true," replied Dave.

"What's the programme?" inquired Hiram, "for I see you don't intend to give up."

"Not until I master the Reliance, just as I did the Baby Racer," declared Dave. "That upset was necessary, I guess, to teach me that I must drive on just as little surface as possible in speeding, and make the wings do one half the work."

"Then you are going to try again?" questioned Hiram.

"Yes, Hiram. The waves aren't so choppy now, and the wind has gone down a good deal."

"It's pretty late for much of a run," replied Hiram.

"Oh, we can make the end of the lake and back inside of an hour."

"Well, I'm always ready—with you," laughed Hiram gaily.

From the start this time Dave knew that he had a better grasp of the mechanism than on his first trial. The Reliance behaved splendidly. Once clear of shore obstructions and sandbars, they must have run a stretch at nearly forty miles an hour.

Sand Point, at the rounding end of the great lake, was reached without a mishap. Dave did not wait to try any maneuvering for a crowd that had gathered to watch the Reliance.

"Straight home," he observed, as they made the turn.

"It's time, I'm thinking," said Hiram.

A squall had come up, and the dimness of coming eventide had already spread over the water, but there was no rain. In fact, it had turned too cold for that. A fine baffling mist was falling, however, and this was condensing into a heavy fog.

"Not much to see, eh?" propounded Dave, as they got clear of the shore. "I shouldn't like to run into some stray craft."

It was something of a strain on Dave, the present situation. No air signal had yet been placed on the Reliance, nor was its lighting apparatus installed.

The darkness increased, and the fog became almost an impenetrable shroud.

"What was that?" shouted out Hiram sharply, as there was a heavy jarring shock.

"Grazed a rock, I think," replied Dave. "I don't like this a bit.

If I knew my bearings, I'd run straight ashore."

"Do it, anyway, Dave," advised Hiram. "We don't want to wreck the

Reliance on her first trip."

Dave gave the wheel a turn. Just then a distinct yell rang out across the muggy waters, and then, in rapid succession, seven quick, snappy explosions.

CHAPTER VII

A RESCUE IN THE FOG

"What do your suppose that was?" inquired Hiram excitedly.

"It was kind of startling," said Dave.

"Listen."

With the power shut off, the hydroplane drifted, Dave checking its slack running. They were now in a dense fog; with night fast coming on. For the moment everything was still. Then there rang through the misty space one word:

"Help!"

"It was in that direction," said Hiram quickly, pointing.

"I think so, too," nodded Dave, "and not far away."

"What could have happened? Those shots?"

"Probably fired to call assistance."

"If you could speed up the hydroplane a little—"

"I would have to get the starter in use, and we might run into something. Hello! Hello! Hello!" Dave shouted loudly. There was a speedy reply.

"Here! Hello! this wa-aa-ay!"

"That's a man's voice, and he's right near to us," declared Hiram, leaning forward and peering through the mist. "Hey, there!"

"I see you. Good!"

There was a tilt of the machine. The person in the water had seized one of the wing stays.

"Careful, there," ordered Dave. "Don't cling to that wing or bear it down."

"I can't hold out."

Dave cautiously edged from his seat towards a form now plainly visible. It was that of a man about thirty years of age.

It was no easy task to take the man aboard. One of his hands was useless. He seemed in pain and half choked with water he had swallowed.

Hiram gave up his seat to the rescued man, who sank back as if overcome with faintness and exhaustion. Hiram himself found a resting place on the platform supporting the two seats.

"Is there anybody else in trouble?" Dave asked of their passenger.

"No, no," replied the man. "The launch is gone up. Get me to land quick as you can. I'm afraid my arm is broken. It pains me terribly. I must get to a surgeon soon as possible."

Dave got the hydroplane under way again.

He was fortunate in striking a course that brought them back to the boat house in about an hour's time.

The rescued man was somewhat revived by this time, and when the hydroplane was safely housed, Dave took his arm and piloted the way from the beach.

"It is less than half a mile to the hangars," the young aviator explained. "When we get there we can find an automobile to take you into town."

"It was when my launch struck a rock that I hurt my arm," the man explained.

"Were you on board alone?" asked the curious Hiram.

"Yes. I was driving ahead full speed, to get ashore out of the fog. I heard your machine, and was afraid I'd get run into. My launch ran into a reef with terrific force. I was thrown against it bulkhead, arm sprained or broken, nearly stunned, and then into the water."

"But the launch, Mister?" questioned the interested Hiram anxiously.

"Smashed. I don't know if I could locate it again in the fog. I couldn't use my hurt arm, and I fired my revolver, yelled, and gave up when your machine came along."

"Where did you come from, Mister?" pressed the persistent Hiram.

"Why—well, I came from up north. Own a launch. Had some business this way, and got well on my way till the craft struck."

Dave noticed as the man spoke that it was in a hesitating, evasive way. He seemed anxious to change the conversation, for he said:

"You are taking me to the Columbus aero field?"

"Yes, we belong there," answered Dave.

"Some people there named Dawson?"

"Yes, father and son."

"That's it. Here, now?"

"Oh, yes, they follow the different meets."

"Why, then, say," observed the man, "if you will just get me up against them, I shall be pleased. You see, they're friends of mine. They'll take care of me."

Dave gave the man a look. Hiram pulled a face at him behind his back. That settled it with Hiram. In his mind he was sure that anybody who knew the Dawsons in a friendly way could not possibly amount to much.

The man did not mention his name. He seemed to care nothing whatever for the fate of the launch. He barely thanked Dave, as, reaching the aero grounds, our hero led him near to the headquarters of the man for whom the Dawsons were working.

"You'll find your friends over there," he said.

"All right," nodded the man he had rescued. "Lucky I met you.

Thanks."

"Say, Dave Dashaway, now what do you think of that!" burst out

Hiram, as the man got out of earshot.

"Think of what, Hiram?" inquired the young aviator.

"Friend of the Dawsons!"

"Well, they've got to know somebody, haven't they?"

"That's so, but I don't like the fellow you rescued."

"Why not, Hiram?"

"Did you notice the way he hesitated when we asked him where he had come from?"

"Yes."

"And about that launch? He didn't seem to care what had become of it."

"Maybe it didn't belong to him."

"Well, anyway, hadn't he ought to have some concern about other folks' property?"

Dave did not reply. He had his own ideas and opinion of the rescued man. He was due for a public exhibition of the Reliance the next day, and dismissed the incident from his mind as he got back to the Baby Racer hangar.

Mr. King was to make a non-stop race also, and there was plenty of detail to attend to at the Aegis headquarters as well.

That was a busy, exciting day, the one following. The Aegis and her competitors got started by ten o'clock. There was a varied programme from eleven to one. At three o'clock Dave made his run with the hydroplane.

Two other machines engaged in the contest, but not only were they of inferior make, but their operators were clumsy and not up to standard.

Dave won considerable praise. The Reliance made a beautiful run, and he felicitated himself that he had got onto the knack of running it right.

"I don't believe much in hydroplanes," old Grimshaw observed to him as he accompanied Dave back to the aero grounds, "but I believe in you, and I will say you made a clever showing."

"Wait till the Interstate folks send on their latest improved aero-hydroplane, Mr. Grimshaw," said Dave. "You'll see some fine work then."

"There's your friend, young Dobbs," remarked Grimshaw.

Dave saw Hiram on a run, headed towards them. He came up breathless.

"Some one at the hangar to see you, Dave," he reported.

"Who is it, Hiram?"

"He says he's a United States revenue officer."

"Hello!" spoke Grimshaw, "I hope your hydroplane hasn't got you into any trouble running up against the government."

"Oh, I think not," replied Dave with a smile.

"It's a long story and a big story, Dave," replied Hiram. "You know the man you rescued he lake yesterday?"

"Yes, Hiram."

"Well, it turns out that he is a notorious smuggler and the government is looking for him."

CHAPTER VIII

A PUZZLING DISAPPEARANCE

Dave hurried his steps. Old Grimshaw turned off at the Aegis headquarters. Hiram led his companion by a short cut to the Baby Racer hangar.

On a campstool inside the tent where the boys slept, Dave found a keen-eyed, hatchet-faced man. He sat stiff as a poker, and seemed to pierce Dave through and through with his glance as he looked him over critically.

"Dashaway, yes?" he interrogated, and as Dave bowed assent he added: "Thought I'd wait and see you, although our young friend here has been pretty dear."

"About what?" asked Dave.

"Ridgely."

"Who is he?"

"The man you rescued from the lake last evening. As I have told your friend, the man is a bad one, and we have chased him up and down the lakes clear from Detroit."

"He is a criminal, then?"

"A smuggler. He has outwitted the revenue officers for some time. His last specialty was running Chinese emigrants over the border. When he learned the chase was on, he stole a launch and scudded for other waters. He had the name and color of the launch changed. Why he came to Columbus we don't know."

"To see some people named Dawson, he said."

"Yes, they appear to be fiends."

"Can't Jerry Dawson tell you anything about him?" asked Dave.

"No."

"For a very good reason."

"And what is at?"

"Dawsons left last night."

"Left—left the meet?" exclaimed Dave in surprise.

"Yes, bag and baggage."

"That puzzles me," said Dave.

"It baffles us," observed the revenue officer, "for they have left no clew to their future whereabouts."

"Won't Jerry's employer tell you?"

"He says he can't. Professes to be quite at sea as to the meaning of their sudden departure. Angry, too, for it seems they had a contract in the service."

"I wouldn't believe him," broke in Hiram. "Anybody respectable about the meet can tell you that he is not to be trusted."

"Well, the Dawsons are gone and Ridgely went away with them," said the revenue officer definitely. "I fancied you might give me some hint that might help me, Dashaway, as to their antecedents, friends."

"I'm a new one in the aviation line," said Dave. "I found them in the business when I joined it, only a few weeks ago."

"Well, I understand you are two pretty keen young fellows," said the officer, "I'm going to leave you my card. There it is."

Dave glanced at the bit of pasteboard his visitor extended. It bore simply a name: "James Price."

"If you get the faintest clew to Ridgely or the Dawsons," continued Mr. Price, "wire the secret service bureau at Chicago. I will arrange so that I shall be advised at once."

"I will do what I can for you, Mr. Price," promised Dave.

"All right, and send in any reasonable bill you like for your service. We feel certain that this, Ridgely, driven from one district, will begin operations in another. Then, too, from what I learn these Dawsons are not above engaging in of off-color schemes."

"They aren't!" cried Hiram. "If they had stayed, Mr. King said they'd be barred from the meets in a few days."

"Well, help me all you can."

"Queer, isn't it?" spoke Hiram, as the revenue officer left them.

"It is a rather strange proceeding," admitted Dave.

At five o'clock that afternoon the two friends were down at the south pylons awaiting the coming in of the machines engaged in the non-stop race. A great crowd was gathered, for according to estimated schedules some of the monoplanes would be due within the coming half hour.

"If it's the Aegis first," spoke Hiram, "it makes three winning stunts for Mr. King in two days."

A sort of instantaneous flutter pervaded the people as some word starting from the judge's stand passed electrically through the crowd.

"They've sighted something," shouted an excited spectator.

"Yes, there's one of the airships," added a quick voice.

"I see it!"

"There's another!"

"Hurrah!"

Hiram stood looking up into the sky, fairly trembling with suspense.

A man standing by Dave had a field glass.

"I make out two," he spoke to an inquirer at his side.

"I think I can tell you who they are if you'll give me your glass for a minute," said Dave.

"Certainly," replied the man.

"What is it, Dave?" cried Hiram, as, watching the face of his comrade closely, he discerned an intense expression upon it.

"Aegis in the lead—" began Dave, lowering the field glass.

"Aegis in the lead!" ran from the spot in receding echoes as the news passed down the line.

"That's King's craft."

"I knew it!"

"Butterfly a close second," reported Dave.

"There's another one!"

"And another!"

"See them come!" cried an excited old farmer. "Say, it beats the electric cars down at Poseyville!"

The field was in a wild flutter. The contesting aircraft came nearer and nearer. Finally Hiram could make out the Aegis fully a mile in the lead, the wings set for a drop straight beyond the south pylon.

"He's won—Mr. King has won!" he shouted again and again, fairly dancing up and down.

The crowd surged towards the landing point as the Aegis gracefully sailed to earth, ran a stopping course, and Robert King stepped out amid the frantic cheers of his friends and admiring spectators in general.

The great aviator looked please and proud. Old Grimshaw trotted at his side on the way to the Aegis hangar.

"Say, you're taking about everything there is in sight," he remarked, with one of his grim chuckles.

"I've run the limit on the set spurts, I guess," replied the expert airman. "I'm going to look, for something better."

"What is there that's better than these famous stunts of yours, Mr.

King?" inquired Hiram.

"A record beater of some account," was the quick response.

"Record breaker of what?" pressed the persistent Hiram.

"Well," said Mr. King with an animated sparkle in his eye, "you and Dashaway come down to the hangar this evening, and I'll tell you all about it."

CHAPTER IX

A GIANT AIRSHIP

Dave Dashaway and his friend were promptly on hand at the Aegis hangar at eight o'clock that evening.

Usually the boys took their meals with Mr. King. A group of the airman's admirers, however, had insisted on a special dinner at a hotel just outside the grounds. Hiram piloted the way for Dave to the restaurant on the field. He had worked for the man having it in charge, and the best meal possible was set out for them free of charge.

They found Mr. King in the little partitioned off room of the Aegis hangar which he used as an office. The airman sat before a desk littered up with a variety of papers. One of these Dave noticed as he entered, was a detailed drawing of an immense airship.

"Oh, arrived, eh?" spoke the aviator with a pleasant smile, as the boys came into view. "Glad of it. Get comfortable seats and we'll have a little chat."

The boys settled themselves in camp chairs, Mr. King closed the door of the apartment and sat down again. Hiram regarded him eagerly and expectantly.

"I've got something to tell you, lads," began the airman, after a brief thoughtful pause. "This is business, and of course you will be wise enough to treat it confidentially."

"I love to keep secrets," declared the ardent Hiram, and Dave smiled and nodded assent to the sentiment.

"I have been thinking and planning for a big event for some time," continued Mr. King.

"As how, now?" asked Hiram, devoured with suspense.

"Well, in the first place I propose to build a giant airship."

"I know," said Hiram. "A big passenger monoplane."

"No," interrupted the aviator. "What I want is a dirigible airship."

"Pshaw! only a balloon!" remarked Hiram disappointedly.

"Not at all," corrected the good-natured airman. "Except for the self-sustaining power, it will be constructed on the best aeroplane principles. I have been working on it for some months, and only yesterday I got figures on the machine."

"What is it for, Mr. King?" submitted the inquisitive Hiram, "exhibitions?"

"No. It's first big feat is to cross the Atlantic."

"Cross the Atlantic Ocean!" almost gasped the excited Hiram.

"Cross the Atlantic!" repeated Dave, in a startled yet thoughtful manner.

He sat looking fixedly at the aviator as if fascinated. The novelty, the immensity of the proposition, stunned Dave.

"Can it be done?" he asked in a low, intense tone, vast dreams running through his mind a lightning speed.

"According to my calculations, yes," replied Mr. King definitely. "Oh, it is no new idea with me. The project has been the constant ideal of every advanced airman. It has got to come to that, if aeronautics is the progressive science we enthusiasts believe it to be."

"I would like to be the first one to win such a triumph," said Dave.

"Yes, the first one gets the fame," said the airman. "The prize, too. If such an experiment was rationally started I believe the profession and its backers would put up a small fortune to go to the successful winner. Now, boys, I have great confidence in you. What has held me back has been the lack of capital."

"Say, Mr. King," broke in Hiram impetuously, "I've got nearly thirty dollars saved up, and Dave—"

"It will take bigger amounts than we three put together can earn just to get the plans of the giant airship on paper," said Mr. King, with an indulgent smile at his loyal young friends. "If I go to any regular aero promoters they will want all the proceeds. I can raise a few thousand dollars myself and do as much more among my friends but, all put together, the amount wouldn't make even a beginning."

"How much will it take, Mr. King?" asked Dave seriously.

"At least twenty-five thousand dollars."

"Whew!" whistled Hiram.

"It's no child's play. It's a big risk, and there's no doing it half way," declared Mr. King. "Last night while I was planning over it, a sudden idea came to me. Dashaway, you remember that fellow who stole my watch and money and medal from you?"

"You mean the young thief who called himself Briggs, and then

Gregg?"

"Exactly."

"Yes, Mr. King."

"And how he used some letters sent to your father from a great friend of his?"

"Mr. Dale?" nodded Dave, wondering what all this had to do with the giant airship scheme.

"Well, as you know, that young scamp, Gregg, had gone to Mr. Dale, who had never seen you, and by means of the letters stolen from you made him believe that he was the son of his old friend. So delighted was Mr. Dale, that he practically adopted young Gregg. In fact, he was on the point of making the pretended Dave Dashaway heir to all his fortune."

"You told me about that," said Dave.

"When we left Dayton to come here, we had to make a hurried jump to fill our contract, as you know. I let Gregg go, after recovering my stolen property from him, but I got a written confession of his bold imposture, first. You know my plan was for you and me to go where Mr. Dale lives, and introduce him to the real Dave Dashaway. You see, although I have managed to scare that old tyrant guardian of yours, Silas Warner, into leaving you alone, I feared he might work some trick to get you back in his clutches again."

"I've thought a good deal about that lately," said Dave.

"My plan was to have this Mr. Dale go to Brookville, show up Warner, and apply for your guardianship."

"Yes, then I would feel safe," said Dave.

"Well, Mr. Dale, having been an old balloonist, would probably not object to your remaining in the same line of business in which your father was famous."

"I should think he would be pleased," remarked Hiram, who was always interested and active in any conversation going on.

"I counted on that," resumed the aviator. "At all events, not being able to go or send Dave to Warrenton to meet this Mr. Dale, I wrote to a friend of mine who lives at Warrenton. I told him the whole story, instructing him to inform Mr. Dale, so if this Gregg came around again, he would be ready to treat him as an imposter. My friend wrote me only yesterday that Mr. Dale was off on an automobile trip, and might not be back for a day or two. He said that Mr. Dale was a very lonely old bachelor. He had been delighted to take up Gregg, believing him to be the son of his old balloonist comrade, so you would, be sure to receive a really grand welcome, Dave."

"I'm glad of that," said Dave, filled with deep gratitude as he contrasted his present circumstances with his former forlorn condition.

"Now then, to business," continued Mr. King briskly. "I don't want to 'work' anybody with my personal schemes, but I see a chance to put my giant airship project on its feet."

"Why," cried Dave brightly, "you mean to interest Mr. Dale?"

"That's just what I do mean," assented the aviator.

Dave rose to his feet, excited and pleased.

"Mr. King," he said earnestly, "I not only would do all I could to have Mr. Dale join you, but I feel sure he would be glad to take an interest in your plan."

"It's worth trying, anyway," responded the airman. "I'm going to go by rail to Warrenton to-morrow, in the hope of finding Mr. Dale at home. I shall send you to him later."

"All this isn't grand, or exciting, or anything of that sort, is it, now!" ejaculated Hiram, as Dave and he returned to the Baby Racer hangar.

"I hope Mr. King's plans come out, all right," responded Dave. "I'll do a good deal to repay him for all he has done for me."

"And me, too," echoed Hiram. "He's a fine fellow!"

Mr. King departed on his journey the next day. Dave was not on the programme, so he practiced some with the hydroplane. Coming home for dinner, he found a letter from the Interstate people.

They were cheery and optimistic over the completion of their new

model aero-hydroplane. It had been tested and worked splendidly.

The company stated that they would ship the machine to the meet at

Columbus two days later.

Dave told Hiram about the machine, and the hitter was in a fever of expectation over its anticipated arrival.

The boys were eating their supper at the King hangar later in the day, when a telegraph messenger appeared.

"Message for Mr. Dave Dashaway," he said. "I'm your man," replied

Dave.

He signed for the message, tore open the envelope, and glanced rapidly over the enclosure. His face clouded as he did so, for the message was from his employers, the Interstate Aero Company, and it read:

"Cancel all dates. Come on at once. Trouble."

CHAPTER X

SOMETHING WRONG

"What is it, Dave?" inquired Hiram, tracing a sudden seriousness in the manner of his comrade.

Dave did not reply. With a thoughtful air he passed the telegram to

Hiram.

"Wonder what's up?" queried the latter.

"I can't imagine," said Dave.

"They tell you to cancel your dates," went on Hiram, looking very much worried.

"Yes, that's what bothers me," replied Dave.

"And to come on to the factory at once."

"Perhaps they want to pay me off and let me go," suggested Dave, pretending to smile.

"Don't take any trouble on your mind on that score," cried Hiram. "They'd search a long time before they'd find a better demonstrator than you are."

"Thank you Hiram," said Dave. "The telegram is plain."

"Yes, cancel all dates."

"That's easy, I have nothing on the programme for the rest of the week."

"There's the aero-hydroplane stunt."

"But the machine hasn't arrived."

"That's so."

"Let's go down and see Grimshaw. I want to talk to him about this," said Dave.

They found the airman at the Aegis hangar. Dave read him the telegram. Grimshaw looked bothered.

"Too bad, when things are going so finely for you," he remarked.

"I wish Mr. King was here," said Dave, "but he probably won't be until tomorrow."

"Hardly, I should judge, from what he said," replied Grimshaw.

"I had better start right off for the Interstate plant."

"Yes. I would do that if I were you," advised Grimshaw.

"I wish you would see the managers and explain about this," continued Dave.

"Suppose the Drifter comes Dave?" asked Hiram.

The Drifter was the name of the new model aero-hydroplane concerning which Dave had received a letter from the Interstate people that day, but written the day previous.

"I'll see that it is handled all right," promised Grimshaw.

"Tell Mr. King I will wire him just as soon as I learn what's up," said Dave. "You'll look after the Racer and the hydroplane, won't you, Hiram?"

"Surely I will," pledged Hiram.

Dave returned to his own quarters and packed a small hand bag. Hiram went to the railroad depot with him. They had to wait two hours for a south-bound train.

The factory of the Interstate Aero Company was located at a city in

Ohio. It was over three hundred miles from Columbus. The train

Dave was on arrived at a junction about daylight the next morning.

There he had to wait for a train on another road.

He had slept a few hours and got his breakfast at the depot restaurant. According to schedule he would reach the Interstate plant about ten O'clock in the morning.

Dave had been looking out of the car window enjoying the scenery and thinking over affairs in general, when he chanced to direct his gaze at a newspaper the man in the forward seat was reading. A glaring head line had caught his eye: "A Burglar In The Clouds."

Anything suggestive of the air was of interest to the young aviator. He wondered what the item might refer to. Dave leaned over to try to scan the body matter of the article, when the locomotive whistled and the train slowed up for a station. The man in front of him shoved the newspaper into his pocket to leave the train. Then the incident drifted from the youth's mind.

Dave reached Bolton on schedule time. An inquiry directed him to the extensive works of the Interstate Aeroplane Company. He found it to be a very large plant. The company, besides manufacturing aircraft, also turned out automobiles.

Past the entrance gates of the big establishment, Dave became at once interested in a large building bearing the sign "Aerodrome." He could not resist the impulse to enter it. Then he found himself going from section to section, viewing the splendid assortment of aircraft on exhibition and for sale.

To a devotee of aeronautics the display was most fascinating. There were monoplanes, biplanes, and hydroplanes. In one section were samples of the various accessories of the craft. Dave was looking over a splendid passenger monoplane when some one hailed him.

"Dashaway—say, we've been expecting you."

Dave turned to face the man who had been sent on by the Interstate people to drill him in the use of the hydroplane at Columbus.

"Yes," nodded Dave, "I got a hurry call wire, and came on at once."

"Seen the manager?"

"Not yet. I drifted in here and lost myself among so many beauties.

I don't see the new hydro-aeroplane."

A quick shade came over the face of Dave's companion.

"No," he hesitatingly replied.

"Has it been shipped to Columbus yet?" inquired Dave.

"Why—that is, I guess I had better let the manager tell you about the machine."

Dave noticed a singular constraint in the manner of his companion.

"Come along, I'll introduce you," volunteered the latter.

Dave accompanied his guide from the aerodrome. They passed several large factory buildings. In their center was a small one story brick structure labeled "Office."

Dave had never met the manager of the Interstate Company. He had transacted all his business with the agent of the company and the hydroplane expert. His companion led him past a row of desks occupied by clerks and stenographers and into a neatly furnished office.

"Here is Dashaway, Mr. Randolph," he said.

A fine looking man writing at a desk wheeled quickly in his chair. He arose to his feet with a pleasant smile and shook Dave's hand in a welcoming way.

"I am glad to meet you," he spoke. "You received our telegram?"

"Yes, sir, and came on at once."

"I suppose you know why we sent for you?" questioned the manager.

"Why, no, sir," replied Dave.

"We tried to keep our loss a secret," proceeded the manager, "but the newspapers got hold of it."

Dave recalled the newspaper heading he had glanced at, "A Burglar In

The Clouds," and wondered if that had anything to do with the case.

"I have not read a newspaper since leaving Columbus last night," said Dave.

"Well," explained the manager of the Interstate Company, "our new model aero-hydroplane his been stolen."

CHAPTER XI

"N. A. L."

"Stolen!" exclaimed Dave, in dismay.

"It startles you?" spoke the manager of the Interstate Aeroplane concern. "So it did us."

"But—"

"You are mystified—unusual occurrence rather. You can follow the track of a stolen automobile. But when it comes to pursuing an airship, you won't find many familiar roads in the clouds."

"How did it happen?" inquired Dave.

"Why, we had tested the machine and it was to have been shipped to you yesterday. The day before, our expert made a very fine and satisfactory demonstration. The tanks were full, everything in perfect shape for another spurt early yesterday morning. During the night some one scaled the fence, evaded the watchman, and broke into the aerodrome."

"It must have been some one familiar with the place here," suggested

Dave.

"We don't know that. It is certain, though, that they knew all about airships."

"Why so?"

"Because from the trail they left we could trace where they ran the machine outside. They gauged its ground run just right. They must have put on the muffler, for the watchman heard no sounds. Then they flew away."

"Do you suspect anybody?" questioned Dave.

"No."

"Could it have been a business rival?"

"Scarcely. We have some hard competitors, but we have canvassed the situation and do not believe they could afford to mix up in a deliberate steal."

"It is strange," commented Dave, in a musing tone.

"Our belief is that the Drifter was selected as the nearest and highest type of aircraft in existence. The people who stole it did so with some definite purpose in view."

"What could that purpose be?" asked Dave.

"We cannot as yet decide. One thing is certain—they will not venture to use it at any of the aero meets."

"Then they must design to take it to a distance."

"Of course."

"You have no trace of it?" asked Dave.

"None whatever. We can account for that, however. The night was dark, they started out when everybody was asleep, and they could have gone in one certain direction and struck a positive wilderness in a few hours time."

"You mean north?"

"Among the pineries, yes."

"Or over the Canadian border?"

"Exactly."

Dave sat silent and thoughtful for some moments. The situation was a novel one. He had never heard of any one stealing an airship before. The Interstate manager aroused him from his reverie with the words:

"We sent for you, Dashaway, because you are our most active man in the field."

"That sounds pretty grand for a young fellow like me," returned Dave with a smile, and flushing up, too.

"We gage out men by what they do," replied Mr. Randolph in a matter-of-fact tone. "We have found blood the best in our business. You have made good, Dashaway."

"Thank you, sir."

"Mr. King said you were the most promising aviator in the field."

"Oh, he is always saying something good about me."

"You proved it in your ideal work with the Baby Racer."

"Who wouldn't, with any pride and that perfect machine?" challenged Dave.

"That dash of yours after that Lyon order when you outwitted the

Star people was simply brilliant. It showed your loyalty to us.

The newspapers have given your hydroplane work so far the biggest

kind of a send off."

Dave was silent. He looked modest and embarrassed at all this praise. He could not, however, feel otherwise than pleased at all these eulogies bestowed upon him.

"The Drifter has got to be found," resumed the manager. "It is our first perfected model, and we can hardly build its counterpart in time for full seasonal exhibitions. We think you are the man to find it, Dashaway."

"Oh, Mr. Randolph," said Dave with a slight start.

"I am expressing the opinion of the head men in the company here, who knew your good record. You are young, ambitious, a capable airman, and above all you are loyal to the interest of your employers."

"I should hope it," exclaimed Dave, roused up to genuine emotion. "Just think—you picked me out, a mere boy, and trusted me. And see what you helped me do, already!"

"Exactly," interrupted Mr. Randolph quickly. "That is just the point—you've outdone some of the veterans in the service and jumped to a high place in a bound. That's why we trust you."

"I don't know about what you propose, though," said Dave, sobering down.

"Yes, it's a pretty hard task to set. We're all at sea."

"So am I," admitted Dave.

"Put those keen wits of yours at work, Dashaway," urged the manager encouragingly. "I know after thinking this affair over you'll be ready to suggest something."

"Well, all airmen should know of the theft of the Drifter, and be on the lookout."

"We notified every association and meet in the country after we found that the newspapers had got onto the theft. That advertises it widely. The persons, however, who stole the Drifter knew that would come about. Rest assured of on point, therefore—they won't stay within range of possible identification any longer than they can help."

"That's so," acknowledged Dave musingly.

"The company wishes you to take charge of a search for the Drifter," went on Mr. Randolph. "Any machine we own, half a dozen of them if you like, are at your disposal. You may proceed regardless of the expense. If Mr. King could be induced to assist—"

"I think he is under contract clear up to the end of the season," explained Dave.

"Sorry for that, but he is such a good friend to you and to us, and

I fancy he would gladly cooperate with advice and direction."

"Yes, indeed," assented Dave.

"We owe you a good deal more than your contract income already, Dashaway," said the manager. "I don't think there's an aviator living ever had a finer settlement than you will have if you succeed in running down the Drifter."

"I'll try," said Dave.

"That's capital."

"Give me a few hours to think it over," suggested Dave.

The young aviator left the Interstate plant very thoughtful and serious. Dave decided that he had assumed a big responsibility. He seemed to feel an actual ponderous weight on his young shoulders.

A score of theories ran riot through his mind its to the motive for the theft of the Drifter. Then he decided that it must be some professional who had done the act. It was hard to fathom the ultimate plans of such an abstractor, who would not dare to use the machine in any public way and could scarcely sell it.

"It's a puzzle, a big, worrying poser," said Dave, walking slowly from the factory grounds.

About half a mile city-wards from the plant Dave passed through a square devoted to public park purposes. He sat down on a tree-shaded rustic bench. There, alone, quiet and undisturbed, he set his wits at work.

Whoever it was who had committed the theft must have been a professional airman. Dave formulated a plan to ask Mr. Randolph if anybody in Bolton, or any employee of the plant was missing. In case this was not discovered then some stranger must have come to Bolton. There might be a trace found of the party at some of the hotels.

"There's a bit of detective work to do by some one besides myself," decided Dave. "I'm going to suggest this plan to Mr. Randolph."

"Hello, boss," spoke an approaching voice as Dave got up to return to the plant.

He observed a man he had noticed on a bench directly opposite to the one he had occupied sidling towards him. The fellow was ragged and trampish looking. There was a queer leer in his face and his eyes were fixed on the coat Dave wore.

"Well, what is it?" inquired Dave.

"Excuse a question, matey?"

"Oh, that's all right."

"Noticed a badge you're wearing," said the tramp.

"Oh, that?" spoke Dave lifting his hand to his coat lapel, and wondering at the man been so observant.

"Yes—N. A. L.," nodded the tramp.

Dave eyed the speaker keenly. At the distance he was, it was doubtful that he could have dearly made out the monogram, yet he named the letters glibly and correctly.

"N. A. L." stood for the National Aero League. Dave was not a member and neither was Hiram Dobbs. Mr. King was and during the meets it had become the custom with professionals to furnish their assistants with duplicate badges, which enabled them to enter and leave the aero grounds unchallenged by the gateman, and ticket takers.

"You must have pretty good eyes to make out those letters on that badge at a distance," said Dave.

"I've seen them before," readily explained the tramp.

"Oh, you have?"

"Yes, and I've got a badge for sale just like the one you're wearing."

CHAPTER XII

DAVE'S DISCOVERIES

"You have got a badge like mine for sale, you say?" exclaimed Dave.

"That's so," bobbed the tramp with a grin.

"Where did you get it?"

"That don't go with the sale, but I didn't steal it."

"You found it, I suppose?" suggested Dave.

"Well, you might call it so." The man drew from his pocket a badge which was the exact counterpart of that worn by the young aviator.

"Let me have a look at it," said Dave.

"No, sir."

"Why not?"

"You can see what it is, can't you? I don't want to get into trouble, boss."

"I'm not going to get you into any trouble," declared Dave.

"Then why do you want to look at the badge? It's no different from yours, is it?"

"Are there no marks on it?"

"Why, I didn't notice. Say, yes, there are," announced the tramp, scrutinizing the little piece of metal on the back of the badge. "Looks like T. O."

Dave put his hand in his pocket.

"What do you want for it?" he asked.

Evidently the tramp was about to say "fifteen cents." He shrewdly, however, observed an interested if not an eager expression on Dave's face, arid added:

"—ty cents."

"It's yours," replied Dave, promptly producing the coin. "Wh-e-w!"

Dave stared, started and gave utterance to a prolonged whistle. He came to his feet with a shock. Upon the rear plate of the badge were scratched two letters, indeed—but the tramp had read them wrong. As read by Dave they were a mine of information.

Dave's mind ran rapidly. He sat down again on the bench. The tramp grinned broadly as Dave turned an eager and excited face upon him.

"Why," he chuckled, "you're real friendly, aren't you?"

"No trifling," said Dave seriously. "I'll give you a good deal more than fifty cents if you tell me truthfully and right away how you came by that badge."

"How much now?"

"Two dollars."

"The information is yours, Cap," answered the tramp, with an assumed air of grandness. "I found it."

"When?"

"At one o'clock yesterday morning."

"Where?"

"By the fence of the big Fly factory down yonder."

"You mean the Interstate works?"

"That's the place, I guess."

Dave became more interested than ever. He handed a two dollar bill to the tramp without further question.

"Now, my man," he said, "I've been square with you."

"That's right," assented the tramp.

"I want you to tell me all about how you came by that badge."

"Well, boss, I'm troubled with asthma, and have to sleep out of doors nights."

"Go on."

"The police in the city know me moderately well, and I prefer the suburbs."

"Don't fool—give me the facts."

"Night before last I camped down in a grassy spot near the fence of the big Fly factory. It must have been about midnight when I was waked up. I heard somebody say: 'Oh, at take it!'"

"Who was it?"

"A boy about your size."

"What was he doing?" asked Dave.

"He was up on top of the fence. He had climbed up one of the slanting outside supports, I guess. You know there's two rows of barbed wire a-top of the boards. Well, there he was, making a great fuss."

"What about?" inquired Dave.

"The back of his coat was all tangled up in the barbs. He couldn't pull it loose. Then I heard some voices speak on the inside of the fence. There were two men there."

"You think they had got over first?"

"It looked that way. They told the boy to pull out of his coat. He got his arms out, started to untwist the coat, stuck his fingers with the barbs, and tumbled over into the factory yard."

"And then?" pressed Dave eagerly.

"H'm! I went to sleep."

"What! not knowing but what they were burglars?"

"Boss, I never mix up with other people's business, good or bad."

"How did you come to get the badge?"

"Why, when I woke up at sunrise I saw the coat sticking on the fence where the boy had left it. I climbed up and got it. The badge was pinned to it."

"You haven't got the coat on."

"Good reason."

"What's that?"

"Well, my own coat is pretty ragged but it ain't a marker to the way that boy's coat was riddled and torn by them barb wires."

"Didn't you search the coat?"

"Every time that, matey."

"And found—?"

"Humph! nothing."

"Nothing at all?"

"Oh, yes, there was some cigarettes, a stub of a pencil and a card with some marks and writing, on it."

"What did you do with the card?" asked Dave.

"Tossed it into the ditch with the coat."

"Do you remember where?"

"Sure, I do."

"I'll give you another dollar to take me to the spot."

"Say, you're a gold mine to me, Cap. Come ahead."

Dave was doing a good deal of active thinking. More than once, as his companion led way around the high board fence enclosing the Interstate plant, Dave took out the badge he had bought and scrutinized the scratches on its back closely.

'The tramp guided the way across a bleak prairie stretch. Then he followed the dry ditch, until they came to a spot where thick clumps of weeds directly lining the fence suggested a cozy resting and hiding place for any stray wayfarer.

"There's where I was asleep, as I told you," spoke Dave's companion, pointing to a spot where the weeds were somewhat trodden down. "And there's the place where the coat caught. See, there's one or two pieces of the cloth of the coat hanging in the barbs yet."

"Yes, I see," assented Dave. "Now, where did you throw the coat and the things you found In it?"

The tramp moved about from place to place, got in line with the fence support, and looked down into the ditch. He moved along slowly, his eyes on the ground. Finally he stooped down.

"Here's the coat—what there's left of it," he reported. "Here's that card, too. I can't find the pencil."

"Never mind that," replied Dave, extending his hand for the proffered objects.

"I smoked up the cigarettes."

Dave glanced eagerly at the card. He shoved it in a safe pocket.

Then he rolled up the coat and placed it under his arm.

"Very good, very good, indeed," he said.

"Here's that dollar I promised you."

The tramp received the money, beaming all over his face.

"Say," he observed, as he moved on, "if it wasn't that you've made me rich enough to retiree from business for a time, I'd offer to find the owner of that coat and the fellows who were with him."

"I'll do just that," said Dave to himself in a satisfied way.

Then, his hand resting on the card in his pocket, he added:

"What luck!"

CHAPTER XIII

HIRAM DOBBS AND THE BIPLANE

Dave walked straight along the fence. By the shortest route possible he reached the gateway entrance to the factory yard.

The tramp had put nimbly in the opposite direction. He was headed for the nearest business street, where he could spend some of the money that he had earned so easily.

The young aviator was very much excited. He had made certain discoveries that had amazed him. He could not help but mentally rejoice over the strange fortune that had come from his stray meeting with the tramp.

"It's a clew—a sure clew," said Dave to himself. "Now to move just right in this affair and make no mistake."

The youth crossed the grounds of the plant and again entered the office building. He did not wait to announce himself, but, as he reached the door of the manager's room and found it closed, he tapped briskly.

"Come in," spoke Mr. Randolph. "Hello, you, Dashaway?"

"Yes, Sir," bowed Dave, removing his cap.

"You are back soon."

"Sooner than I planned," replied Dave, "But I—"

"You've thought the affair over, I hope?"

"Something more than that, Sir," responded Dave. "I have come to tell you that I think I can be of some service to you about that stolen aero-hydroplane."

"Good for you!"

"I've thought out a plan, Sir," went on Dave. "I feel certain that the people who raided the aerodrome and made off with the Drifter are bound for a distant and unsettled section."

"But why? What benefit can they hope to secure way off from civilization?"

"That we have to guess at and work out," replied Dave. "I will say, Mr. Randolph, that I think I have a faint clew to the disappearance of the airship."

"You don't say so!"

"I shall know more inside of twenty-four hours. In fact, Mr. Randolph, I feel pretty certain that I can soon submit a plan that will satisfy you that I know what I am about."

"We already think that of you, Dashaway."

"And that I can bring results."

"Capital! I knew we were not mistaken in you. Now, see here, I see you have something working in your mind. I don't want to even hamper you by asking what it is."

"I would like to go back to Columbus on the first train, Mr.

Randolph."

"Very well."

"I want to look up some affairs there, consult with Mr. King, and come back here the next day."

"And then?"

"I shall perhaps want to use the very best aircraft you have in your factory."

"To hunt for the Drifter?"

"Yes, Sir."

"Dashaway, the whole plant and everything in it is at your service."

"Thank you, Sir."

"I consider this theft of the Drifter even more important than I at first thought."

"How is that, Mr. Randolph?"

"I have been thinking that if some competitor was concerned in the affair, he might steal and utilize many points in our new model which are not yet protected by patents."

"I feel pretty sure that no business rival had anything to do with the theft," observed the young aviator confidently.

"Well, you work this affair out in your own way. Remember, as I told you, expense is no point whatever. When shall we see you again?"

"To-morrow evening, or the next morning at the latest."

Something in Dave's manner seemed to convince the shrewd manager of the Interstate Aeroplane Company that their young employee was started on the right track. He shook hands cordially with Dave when the latter left the office.

Dave went at once to the railroad depot. He learned that a train left in two hours.

"That will bring me to Columbus before dark," he reflected. "I wonder what Mr. King will say?"

The young aviator had a good deal on his mind, enough to make the average lad impatient. He had, however, learned a hard lesson of discipline with his tyrannical guardian, old Silas Warner. Then, too, since coming under the helpful influence of Mr. King, he had acquired a certain self reliance that now stood him in good stead.

Running an airship took nerve, steadiness of purpose, a definite, concrete way of looking at things. Dave knew in his own mind that the Drifter was each hour speeding farther and farther away from the haunts of men. He recalled the old adage, however, which says "the more haste the less speed," and he determined to stick to the plan he had mentally outlined at the start.

"I'm going to work on this affair slow but sure," he told himself. "I think I can guess where the Drifter is headed for. If I am right, I know that I shall find it."

Dave reached Columbus about dark. He went straight from the depot to the aero grounds. The plan he had formed in his mind took in a talk with Mr. King right away. The Baby Racer hangar, however, was on his way to the Aegis quarters. As he neared it he saw a light in the shed where the little biplane was housed. Dave went to the half open door of the place to find Hiram Dobbs with a lantern puttering about the machine.

"What have you been up to, Hiram?" challenged Dave.

"Why, hello! Got back? Good!" cried Hiram, rushing forward to warmly welcome his best friend.

"Yes, just arrived," answered Dave.

"I've been cleaning up the machine," explained Hiram. "It's old

Grimshaw's fault."

"What is?"

"Taking the Baby Racer out."

"Oh, the machine has been out, then, has it?" remarked Dave.

"Yes, and up. Say, Dave, I made the five hundred feet level. I hope you're not put out. It was a chance to make fifty dollars."

"Fifty dollars?"

"Uh-huh," bobbed Hiram in a broad grin.

"How was that?"

"Why, Grimshaw was piloting a party over the grounds. Rich man and his family-wife, son and two daughters. The youngest one was a daring little miss. She wanted to fly, and would fly. Grimshaw got to bragging about what you had done with the Baby Racer. Well, nothing would do but I must roll the little beauty out."

"That was all right, Hiram," the young aviator hastened to say. "I should always feel that the biplane is safe in your hands."

"Well, finally the father consented to let his daughter try a fly along the ground. I settled her in a comfortable seat, and away we went. I made it a good stiff run, and there was some jolting, but the girl was wild over it. She begged for a second run. We got such a fine start that I lifted about twenty feet in the air."

"And then, of course, she screamed out in fear?" said Dave, with a smile.

"Screamed nothing," dissented Hiram. "She just spoke one delighted 'O-oh!' and then: 'Higher, oh, please keep on going!' Say, Dave, she looked so bright and brave I couldn't help it—Z—I—P!'"

"What does 'Z—I—P!' mean, Hiram?" asked Dave.

"A slide, a swoop, then a circle, another, a shoot upwards, and the girl laughing out, 'Oh, this is just grand!' Her sister shrieked, her mother fainted away, and her father was shaking his cane at us and yelling for us to come back. The Racer did her prettiest in two grand circles of the grounds, and came down light as a feather. The girl jumped out, one big smile. 'Just think of it!' I heard her cry to her sister, 'when I've told my seminary chums that I've been up in a real airship!' Then, seeing that she was safe, I think her folks were just as proud of her exploit as she was. Anyhow, she ran up to her father in a coaxing way, and came back to place a bank note in my hand. When they were gone, and I found that it was a fifty dollar bill, old Grimshaw chuckled and said he had hinted to the party that the regular fee for a ride in an airship was one hundred dollars. I'm mighty glad you're back, Dave."

"Why, you seem to have got along finely without me," said Dave.

"We've missed you, all the same. Where you going, Dave?" asked

Hiram, as his friend moved out of the shed.

"Why, I'm anxious to see Mr. King as soon as I can. I have something very important to talk about with him."

"It's about that rush telegram?"

"Yes, Hiram."

"What did it mean?"

"When we meet with Mr. King you shall, hear all about it, Hiram."

"Well, Mr. King isn't home yet," explained Hiram.

Dave looked disappointed.

"That is," continued Hiram, "he hadn't got back when I was last up at the Aegis hangar."

"When was that?"

"About four o'clock this afternoon. Mr. Grimshaw, though, said he expected him on the six o'clock train."

"We'll go and see if he has returned," said Dave.

They started for the aviator's headquarters. Half the distance covered, they met him coming in search of them. Mr. King looked pale and worried. Dave knew that something had happened to upset him.

"I'm glad you're back, Dashaway," said Mr. King. "Grimshaw told me you had been called to headquarters by the Interstate people. I should have wired you to return right away if you had not returned. Something very important has transpired."

"About Mr. Dale—about my father's old friend, Mr. King?" asked

Dave.

"That's it exactly. Bad news, Dashaway, I'm sorry to say," announced the aviator in a very serious tone.

CHAPTER XIV

THE MISSING AIRCRAFT

The aviator led the way back to the Aegis hangar. Dave saw that Mr. King was not inclined to explain any further until they were off the public course, so he asked no more questions, for the present. Dave had a good deal to tell himself. His mind had been full of it all day. Something in the grave, thoughtful manner of Mr. King, however, caused him to defer his own anxiety and impatience.

When they were inside the comfortable room where the aviator made his office, Mr. King turned to Dave with a very sober face.

"I said I had bad news, Dashaway," he spoke, "and that's no mistake."

"Then you failed to find Mr. Dale at Warrenton?" inquired Dave.

"He has not been there for over a week."

"Why, I thought he lived there?"

"He did. He went away, or was kidnapped, nearly ten days ago."

"Kidnapped?" exclaimed Dave in surprise.

"That's what I think. Mr. Dale lived alone, except for a very old man servant. As near as I can figure it out, that young thief, Gregg, appeared at Warrenton two days after I had him arrested. I did a very foolish thing in dealing with the young scamp."

"You mean letting him go free?" inquired Dave.

"Yes, I feared at the time that I was unwise in not punishing him, to serve as a lesson against more mischief. He acted so scared, though, he helped me get back the property he had stolen from you, he signed a confession telling that he was not the real Dave Dashaway and had imposed on Mr. Dale, so I thought he would proceed to at once make himself very scarce. I felt sure that he would not be able to play any more tricks on Mr. Dale, for I expected that you and I would go the very next day and see this old friend of your father. You know we were rushed from Dayton to the next meet, and had no chance to get to Warrenton and explain matters to Mr. Dale. I blame myself for not sending you at, once to him at the time. As I told you, I wrote to a friend, a lawyer at Warrenton, to learn what I could about Mr. Dale. He reported Mr. Dale was absent on a trip. When I got to Warrenton yesterday and met the old Dale servant, I saw at once that something was wrong."

"How do you mean, Mr. King?" asked Dave quite anxiously.

"Well, I learned that this young scamp, Gregg, had appeared at

Warrenton two days after I let him go."

"Still pretending to be Dave Dashaway?"

"So the old servant says. Gregg and Mr. Dale went away together.
There is no doubt in my mind that Gregg put up a plot to get Mr.
Dale away from Warrenton before we could expose him."

"But he could not keep Mr. Dale away from home forever?"

"No, but he and his accomplices might get the old man to some remote place
and make him a prisoner."

"And force him to give up a lot of money before they let him go."

"Yes, that has been done before," admitted Dave.

"Anyhow, two days alter Mr. Dale left Warrenton, a check passed through
the bank signed by him for one thousand dollars."

Dave was both interested and alarmed.

"Four days ago a check for two thousand dollars arrived. The bank refused
to cash it."

"Why, Mr. King?"

"Because it was a forgery."

"Not Mr. Dale's signature?"

"That's it."

"But where did the checks come from?" inquired Dave.

"From two cities, widely apart. I know the places. It looks to me as if the first
check was given willingly by Mr. Dale. Then he must have become
suspicious, and refused to pay out any more money. The second check was
numbered correctly, and Gregg must have got possession of the old man's
regular check book."

"This is a pretty serious affair, Mr. King," commented Dave.

"It is, and I came straight back here to tell you about it, and then cancel all
my engagements at the meet. I shall start out at once to run down this
Gregg and locate Mr. Dale."

"And I must join you-I see that it is my duty," declared Dave.

"Not at all," responded the aviator definitely. "I have mapped out the best
plan of procedure, and I believe I can run down this business alone in a very
short time."

Dave was really anxious concerning Mr. Dale. He truly believed it his first
duty towards the old friend of his father to do all he could to assist him. For

all that, Dave was relieved to know that he could go on without interruption in service of his employers.

"Yes," proceeded the aviator, "I feel that I have an interest in finding Mr. Dale. In the first place, he is your friend. Next, I feel responsible for letting that young scamp, Gregg, go free. At a selfish motive, I believe that if I succeed in rescuing the old man he will gladly finance my giant airship scheme."

"He surely will, Mr. King," said Dave confidently. "I believe he would help you, anyway. I do hope he can be found."

"I shall not rest until he is," declared the aviator. "Now, Dashaway, I don't want you to take this affair on your mind. If I fail in what I have planned, I will certainly call you into the case. I fancy, from what Hiram here has told me, that you have some important business of your own on hand."

"Yes, that is quite true," replied Dave seriously.

"Are you having some trouble with the Interstate people?" inquired the aviator pointedly.

"Not on my account, I, am glad to say, Mr. King," replied Dave. "There is some trouble, though, for all hands around. It's about the stolen aero-hydroplane, or hydro-aeroplane, they haven't just settled on the exact name."

"The Drifter?"

"Yes, sir."

"I read about that strange case. I suppose it puts you back in your arrangements at the meet here?"

"Not only that, Mr. King," explained Dave, "but it has placed me in a position where I shall have to give up all my engagements for a time."

"Why, you don't say so, Dashaway?" exclaimed the aviator, much disturbed.

"Those are the orders," replied Dave. "I have hurried back to

Columbus purposely, to consult on your helping in a search for the

Drifter."

"Of course that is not possible, now that this Dale affair has come up," said Mr. King. "As to a search for the stolen aircraft, that is going to be no easy task, I'm thinking. Have the Interstate people no theory as to the way the Drifter was stolen, and the motive for the theft?"

"I had better tell you all I know about it, Mr. King."

"Do so, Dashaway."

Dave proceeded to relate his interview with Mr. Randolph, the manager of the Interstate factory. He did not refer just then to his experience with the tramp.

"It's a good deal of a puzzle," commented the aviator. "What is your plan?"

"Why, I expected that I could induce you to take charge of the search. As you cannot, I am thinking of Hiram going back with me to Bolton."

"What's your idea?"

"The Interstate people have offered me their best monoplane to start the chase for the missing Drifter."

"It will be a blind start, Dashaway, without a clew."

"But I have a clew," announced Dave.

"You didn't say so."

"I hadn't come to that yet, Mr. King. I haven't even told the Interstate people. I am pretty certain that the Drifter left Bolton on a due northwest course," and Dave drew from his pocket the card he had got from the tramp.

"Capital!" cried the aviator, becoming very much interested. "If you know that, you have half solved the problem."

"Besides that," went on Dave, producing the duplicate N. A. L. badge, and glancing at the scratched initials on its back, "I know who stole the Drifter."

"What's that?" almost shouted the aviator, springing to his feet, in a great state of excitement.

"Say, Dave, are you sure?" pressed the eager Hiram Dobbs, worked up to fever heat with curiosity and suspense.

"Who was it?" asked Mr. King.

"Jerry Dawson," was Dave Dashaway's reply.

CHAPTER XV

AT THE AERODROME

"That is the machine I want, Mr. Randolph," said Dave Dashaway.

It was two days after the young aviator had told his friends at Columbus the name of the person he suspected of stealing the aero-hydroplane, the Drifter from the Interstate Aeroplane Company.

Now, he and Hiram and the manager of the Interstate plant stood amid the half hundred or more aero machines that comprised the stock of one of the largest factories in that line in the country.

They had left the aero meet at Columbus the evening previous, not, however, until Dave had explained how he came to suspect Jerry Dawson.

"It's simple and plain, Mr. King," the young aviator had said. "The badge I bought from the tramp at Bolton was the property of young Dawson."

"Sure of that, Dashaway?" Mr. King had inquired.

"Oh, yes. The initials are crude, but they certainly stand for 'J.

D.' and not 'T. O.' as the tramp thought."

An inspection of the duplicate badge by both Mr. King and Hiram satisfied them that Dave's theory was correct.

"Another thing," Dave had added—"the coat found on the barb wire top of the factory fence I have seen Jerry wear many a time."

"And the card?" pressed Hiram.

"The card has some scrawls on it, made by Jerry, I think. It shows a sort of rough outline of the upper lake district here. Some arrows show a straight course due northwest. I believe the Drifter was started on its way over the Canadian border."

"And the two men with Jerry?" asked Mr. King.

"I can't figure out that they could be anybody but Jerry's father and the man who left Columbus with them—Ridgely."

"The man the revenue officer was looking for!" exclaimed Hiram.

"The smuggler, as he was called, yes," replied Dave.

Mr. King and Hiram indulged in all kinds of conjectures as to the possible motive of the party of three in stealing the aircraft.

"The way I figure it out," said Mr. King, "is that this Ridgely wanted to get out of the country knowing that the revenue people were dose on his trail."

"Perhaps," agreed Dave thoughtfully. "There's another thing, though."

"What's that?" inquired the interested Hiram.

"His coming all the way around the lakes to find his friends, the Dawsons, looks as though he had some future scheme in view, with an airship a part of it."

"That's so," assented Mr. King. "Well, Dashaway, you have done famously so far in finding out what you have. The Interstate people think the only way to chase the fugitives is with one of their own machines. I don't know anybody better adapted to do just that than yourself."

"Thank you, Mr. King," said Dave modestly

The two boys left Columbus with pretty clear minds. They had a definite purpose in view, and Mr. King, Dave felt sanguine, would do all that the interests of Mr. Dale required while they were gone.

"Say, Dave," spoke Hiram, as they boarded the train bound for

Bolton, "this is just like acting out some story, isn't it?"

"In a way," acquiesced the young aviator, "only there won't be much acting— it will be real, earnest hard work."

"I see that, and I am anxious to do my share," declared Hiram.

"You always are, Hiram," said Dave.

Now, the morning following, the two aviator friends found themselves at the Interstate factory, where both received a warm welcome from Mr. Randolph.

Dave now related to the manager all that he had held back during his first visit to the great plant.

"I say, Dashaway, that's simply wonderful," was Mr. Randolph's enthusiastic comment. "Anybody with the genius to gather up all those clews cannot fail to work out this entire case. We shall soon receive some great reports from you."

"I hope so," said Dave.

"Now then, you and your friend go over to the aerodrome and see which one of our machines there suits you best."

It was after Dave and Hiram had spent the most fascinating half hour of their lives viewing the wonders of mechanism on display, that the manager rejoined them. It was then, too, that Dave reported to him with the words:

"That is the machine I want, Mr. Randolph."

As Dave spoke he pointed to a monoplane of which he had made a close inspection for over ten minutes. The manager burst out into a hearty laugh.

"Well, well!" he cried, clapping Dave on the shoulder in an approving way, "I must say you are certainly a grand judge of monoplanes."

"How is that?" asked Dave.

"You have picked out the best machine in the place."

"Why, I was looking for the best one, wasn't I, Mr. Randolph?" asked the young aviator with a smile.

"It is our new model of the composite hydro-aeroplane," explained the manager. "It's the best standard built in this country—the Monarch II."

"It's easy to see that," responded Dave. "It is the equal of the

Drifter in a great many ways."

"That is true," replied Mr. Randolph. "While it may not be as swift in the water as an all-steel hydro, it is built on the best float system and will sustain a weight of one thousand three hundred pounds."

"And the front elevation and tail are also of the newest type," said

Dave.

"You studied that out, eh? It's a model of lightness as such machines go. The engine is only three hundred pounds, it carries twenty gallons of gasoline, and has a lifting capacity of twelve hundred pounds, giving leeway for a three hundred pound pilot."

"Dave and I wouldn't weigh that together, Mr. Randolph," said Hiram.

"Its simplicity strikes me," remarked Dave.

"Yes," said Mr. Randolph, "and it can be knocked down and reassembled in a hurry. You see, the ailerons never leave their sections and in the planes not a wire is changed. The outriggers fold, keeping them in pairs together, each piece is bent, not buckled, and can be straightened good as new in case of a disarrangement."

The manager went over the entire machine in a speedy but expert way. He saw that all locks on the turnbuckles were fastened, and that the locks had lock washers beneath them. All the movable wires were reinforced with a piece of loose hay wire, and provisions against rust perfected.

Hiram stood mute, but fascinated, as the manager explained in detail the fine points of the Monarch II, as the composite hydro-aeroplane was named.

What interested Dave immensely was a self starting apparatus. This was operated by a handle inserted in a socket, fastened on a special ball ratchet on the large sprocket. Pulling this handle turned the motor over two, sometimes three compressions, and started up the machine without difficulty, Mr. Randolph explained. During the operation the throttle shut down so that the operator might resume his seat and take the levers.

The planes had double covered fabric on top and bottom, tightened at the rear of the planes by lacing. A single lever controlled the elevator and side flaps and there were radical bearings to take both side and end thrusts.

"Tell you, Dashaway," said Mr. Randolph in conclusion, "I'll trust you with the Monarch II because you are something more than a grass-cutting pilot by mail trying to coast a flying machine off the ground."

"I hope to deserve your compliment," laughed the young aviator.

"You've got a horse power engine and planes hard to beat. There are self-priming oil pumps, an auxiliary exhaust, and the machine follows the lines of the lowest gasoline consumption. Remember the triple axis conditions, Dashaway. One controls the fore and aft axis, producing tipping. The second is the vertical axis, producing turning. The third is the lateral axis, producing rising and falling."

"Some one at the office wishes to see Mr. Dashaway," just here interrupted a lad from the plant.

"To see me?" spoke Dave in some surprise.

"Yes, sir. He asked me to give you his card, and said he had come quite a distance to see you."

Dave took the card the lad handed him. He was a little startled, and then curious, as he read the name—

"JAMES PRICE, Revenue Officer."

CHAPTER XVI

THE "MONARCH II"

The manager of the Interstate factory and Dave and Hiram followed the messenger from the plant back to the office.

"The gentleman who wishes to see me," the young aviator explained to

Mr. Randolph, "is the revenue officer I told you about."

"Ah, I think I understand the purpose of his visit, then," said the manager.

Mr. Price was the same keen-faced, ferret-like person he always appeared, as Dave introduced him to the manager.

"I have heard of you from our young friend, Dashaway," said Mr.

Randolph.

"Lucky I ran across him," responded the officer, in his usual short, jerky way. "Lucky to catch you here, too, before you got off, Dashaway."

"Then you came specially to see me?" asked Dave.

"And your friends," replied Mr. Price with a comprehensive wave of his hand. "Mutual interests all around, it seems. You see, I met Mr. King at Columbus after you left," explained the official. "He told me of your remarkable discoveries, Dashaway. You are keener than I, young man. I have been chasing all over the district, and here you get a clew to Ridgely, while I and my men were blundering around."

"If it is really a dew to him, Mr. Price," submitted the young aviator. "You know, it is all a theory so far."

"As the facts stand, I have no doubt from your story that Ridgely is one of the men who ran away with the Drifter," declared the officer.

"Have you fathomed his purpose in taking the air route, Mr. Price?" asked the factory manager.

"Most certainly."

"I am puzzled to guess what it may be."

"Why, it's plain as the nose on your face," said the officer bluntly.

"How is that?"

"You know that this man, Ridgely, is a professional smuggler?"

"So Dashaway has told me."

"We drove him from one point on the border. He has selected another, that's all. He has worn out the old methods of evading the revenue service, so he is adopting new ones. In fact, I rather admire his brilliant originality. Why, I can conceive no situation so ideal as that capture of an airship, and professional operators in his employ."

"Then—"

"I am positive that the Dawsons and Ridgely have made for some obscure point, probably near Lake Superior, and will open up business in the old way, do their work only at night, and I have come on here to ask Dashaway to work in harmony with me."

"Most certainly he will," pledged the factory manager.

"I am after Ridgely, you are after your aircraft. We can work together," pronounced the officer. "I intend to start at once for the Lake Superior district. I shall set my men at work clear along the line and over the border, to try and find a trace of my man. I haven't an airship, though, you must remember, and wouldn't know how to run one if I had. That's where you come in, Dashaway. You search the air, I'll watch the land. What I want to do is to give you a list of points where I or my men can be reached at a moment's notice any time. If we keep in touch with each other, I believe we can land those rascals."

For over an hour after that the officer and Dave had an earnest, confidential chat together. Mr. Price brought out maps, and gave Dave great deal of information as to the smuggling system on the border. In the meantime, Randolph and Hiram again visited the aerodrome. After the revenue officer had departed, Dave came across Hiram looking for him.

"Say, Dave," exclaimed the excited youth, "it's like a new world to me, all this. I declare, I never had such a time in my life. This Mr. Randolph is a prince."

"Fixed things up for us, has he, Hiram?"

"Right royally. He's stocked up that monoplane like a banquet hall. Why, say, if we can keep the Monarch II aloft, we can live like millionaires in an up-to-date hotel for a week to come."

Hiram in his enthusiasm was exaggerating things considerably.

However, when Dave revisited the aerodrome, he found that the clever

Interstate manager had stocked up the aircraft, with every necessity

for safety and comfort he could think of.

The Monarch II was certainly a marvel in its construction and scope. It had been made to accommodate an operator and one, or even two, passengers. The seating space was quite roomy, and there was a handy basket-like compartment, arranged to hold wraps, provisions and duplicate machine parts.

It was late in the afternoon when the Monarch II was rolled out into the broad roomy yard of the factory. Everything was in order for the finest start in the world. Dave had thought out and mapped out every detail of the proposed air voyage. Mr. Randolph personally superintended all the initial arrangements. The starter worked liked a charm. There was no wavering. A turn of the handle, and the magnificent machine spread its wings like some great bird poised for a steady flight.

Hiram gave a great shout of delight. Dave smiled down at the manager proudly.

"Good luck!" cried Mr. Randolph.

Just then the factory whistle sounded out shrilly for quitting time. Workmen appeared at the open windows of the factor. Some came running out into the yard.

The word had gone around that the young aviators were bound on an extraordinary cruise—a search for the stolen airship. A great chorus of ringing hurrahs went up from the crowd.

"It's great, isn't it, Dave?" chuckled the delighted Hiram.

"The Monarch II acts prettily, that's sure," replied the young aviator.

Dave delighted his companion by giving him charge of the barograph readings and attention to some of the minor duties of aviation. The rapid progress of the machine in mid air was exhilarating. The weather conditions were ideal, and Dave had a definite goal in view.

There was not a break in the pleasant twilight journey. The Monarch II fulfilled all expectations and promises. About nine o'clock in the evening the record showed over two hundred miles accomplished, when they descended on a level stretch of prairie near a small bustling city. Here the gasoline supply in the tanks was replenished. The basket had been stored with over a hundred gallons of this in separate packages, without embarrassing the buoyancy of the machine, as the young aviators were far below average operating weight.

"This high living of ours makes and hungry," intimated Hiram, as they finished getting the machine in shape to renew the flight.

"Time for lunch, you think?" proposed Dave with a jolly laugh.

"Here we are."

They selected from the packages in the accommodation basket enough things for a feed. Mr. Randolph had certainly provided for them in a liberal way. The packages produced two kinds of sandwiches, some doughnuts, a cream cakes, cheese, celery and a prime apple pie.

Dave was pleased and proud with their progress thus far on their strange journey. There was a steady but mild head wind, and if he held till daylight the young aviator counted on reaching the first important destination on the route he had mapped out.

His idea was to reach a certain point in the dark. They would then seek a hiding place, or at least seclusion, until evening again, resting through the day. Dave's plan was to travel so that their progress might not be noted and get to the Dawson group through the public prints or by some other avenue, and thus warn them that they were being traced.

There was not a landmark on the route, such as a city, lake or river, that Dave had not memorized, from standard "fly" directories during the past two days. The Drifter, being in the hands of the Dawsons, who knew considerable about aviation, would probably follow the same course. At night it was more difficult to tally off progress than in daylight, but so far Dave felt that he had not deviated from the due northwest course that was to bring him to a certain destination.

For over five hours after lunch and rest the Monarch II kept steadily on its way. Dawn was just breaking when Dave passed a few miles to the west of a town he knew to be Millville. He glanced at Hiram, about to address him. Hiram was fast asleep.

"We will have to get down somewhere near here," decided Dave.

As he changed the course of the aircraft there was a slight jar, and

Hiram woke up.

"Hello!" he cried, "have I been—"

"Asleep at the switch?" smiled Dave. "Yes, but it hasn't needed any attention. We are going to land, Hiram."

Dave knew his bearings, as has been said. His anxiety, however, was to get to cover, so to speak, before the airship was seen by anyone in the vicinity. He soon knew that he had failed in this. Circling about and drifting in trying to select a suitable landing spot, Dave made out rising farmer staring up at the machine from his chicken yard.

A little farther on the driver of a truck wagon, bound town-wards evidently, espied the Monarch II, even in the dim morning light, for he stopped his horses, his face turned in the direction of the machine.

Finally Dave located a spot that suited him. It was where there had been mining going on some period in the past. Some hills shut in the deserted diggings. Several great heaps of ore surrounded a sort of pit, broad and roomy.

"I don't think we can find a better resting place," said Dave, as they reached the ground and he shut off the power.

"Going to stay here all day?" inquired Hiram.

"That is the programme, yes."

"Well, I suppose breakfast is the first move?" asked the young aviator's assistant.

"I'm hungry as a bear," announced Dave.

"So am I," agreed Hiram, and he set at work to explore the accommodation, basket.

Hiram soon had a tempting spread. There was cold ham, a roasted chicken, an abundance of bread and butter, and a two gallon jug of cold coffee.

The boys did full justice to the layout. Then Dave went over the machine, seeing to it that every part was in order.

"I'll have to take a little nap, Hiram," he advised his companion.

"No, a good long one," corrected Hiram.

"If we're going to lay off until night, there isn't much to do. I'll stay awake and keep a look out for anything happening. You see, I had quite a snooze up there in the air."

Dave made a comfortable couch by spreading out some of the wraps found in the accommodation basket. It was after ten o'clock when he woke up. He insisted on Hiram taking a turn on the couch.

"Can't do it. Not a bit sleepy," declared Hiram.

"Well, you can try it while I'm gone," suggested Dave.

"Oh, going somewhere?"

"Yes, to the town. I want to make a few inquiries as to the country around here and ahead of us, and I may wire Mr. Randolph."

"All right, go ahead," replied Hiram. "I'll see that everything is kept trim and safe about the machine."

Dave visited Millville, and posted himself as to certain geographical points in which he was interested. He also sent a brief dispatch to the Interstate people. Provided with some railroad maps, and some fresh rolls from a bakery, he started out to rejoin his chum.

He found Hiram busy burnishing up every bit of metal about the Monarch II. They had their noon lunch. On his way back from town Dave' had noticed a little brook. He was telling Hiram about it, and they were discussing a plan of a plunge and a swim, when Hiram, facing the point where the pit began, sprang suddenly to his feet.

"Hello!" he cried excitedly. "Someone is coming."

"Sure enough," echoed Dave, also arising. "Why, I noticed that man in Millville. Can it be possible that he has followed me? I didn't know it, if he has."

The boys stood motionless, awaiting the coming up of the intruder. He was a brisk, smart looking man. There was something in his sharp way of glancing at things that made Dave think of a lawyer. The stranger came up within a dozen feet of them. Then he halted, took in the flying machine with a grim smile, and then looked the young aviators over from head to foot.

"Reckon I've landed on both feet," he observed, a confident, satisfied drawl in his voice.

"What do you mean by that?" inquired Dave.

"Why, I've been looking out for an airship said to be cruising around this neighborhood. Truck farmer said he saw one early this morning. Then I noticed you in town. I think you'll understand me, young man," continued the stranger, "when I say that I'm on the hunt for a chap about your size running a stolen airship, and whose name is Jerry Dawson."

"Why," exclaimed Dave with a quick start, "so are we!"

CHAPTER XVII

ON THE WING

Hiram stared his hardest at the stranger, Dave's eyes quickened with sudden intelligence. Almost in a flash he took in the situation.

"You just mentioned a name," he said. "I would like to mention another one."

"All right, what?"

"James Price."

"Hello!"

The stranger looked flabbergasted, as the saying goes. He furrowed his brow as if puzzled.

"You have made a mistake," continued Dave. "You think one of us two is Jerry Dawson."

"I did think it, yes," admitted the man, a trifle less self assured than at first.

"Wrong."

"Is that so, now?"

"Yes. You know Mr. Price, don't you?"

"Perhaps I do."

"And you are on the lookout for an airship, but not this machine. Let me explain briefly, and see if we cannot come to an understanding."

Dave surmised that the stranger must be one of the assistants of Mr. Price, the revenue officer. In a very few minutes he knew that this was true. Assured from Dave's talk that he was not the Dawson boy, and that the hydro-aeroplane before him was not the Drifter, the man became very friendly.

It seemed that he was one of the agents of the revenue service. He made his headquarters at Millville, and had received a telegram from Mr. Price the day previous to look out for the stolen airship. This was before Mr. Price had met Dave at Bolton, but immediately after Mr. King at Columbus had told him of the discovery that the Dawsons had made away with the Drifter.

So far as the man knew, none of the many assistants of Mr. Price had found any traces of the missing aero-hydroplane. Dave did not enlighten him as to his plans and destination, for the man's present duties were simply those of a lookout at Millville.

The stranger stayed and chatted with the boys for over two hours, and then went away. Dave had told him that they would not start out again with the

Monarch II until after dark. About six o'clock the man drove up with a wagon.

"Thought you might be getting tired of cold dry fare," he said, "so

I've brought you a real supper for a change."

"Why, say, you're a prince!" cried the impetuous Hiram, as the man lifted a gas oven from the wagon, and then a shallow box, and the contents of both receptacles were revealed.

The oven contained two heaping dishes of lamb chops, and potatoes, still quite warm. From the box the stranger produced all the trimmings for a first class meal.

"This is pretty kind and thoughtful of you," said Dave.

"Nothing too good for friends of Mr. Price," insisted the man.

"Besides, I remember how good the present of a meal has been when

I've got stranded on duty myself."

The speaker, it seemed, had been a member of the Canadian mounted police. The boys whiled the time away interestingly during the next two hours, listening to some of, his exciting experiences with Indians and outlaws in the Winnipeg wilds.

It was just after dark when the Monarch started on the second stage of the journey. Three stops were made during the ensuing six, hours. Dave was very tired and Hiram pretty sleepy, when, at three o'clock in the morning, the machine came to rest on a little reed-covered island in the center of a swampy stretch.

"We may stay here for several days, I don't know exactly how long," the young aviator told his assistant.

"You don't suppose that the Dawsons and the Drifter are anywhere near here, do you?" inquired Hiram.

"Perhaps not, but we are near Ironton, on the American side of Lake

Superior. If Mr. Price's theories are all right, that fellow,

Ridgely, will begin his new operations somewhere in this district."

"I see," nodded Hiram. "What are we to do now—sleep?"

"As much as we like for the next eight or ten hours."

"I'm ready," announced Hiram. "It's been fine and dandy up aloft there, but I notice that when it doesn't make a fellow hungry it does make him good and sleepy."

"All right, we'll bunk down, Hiram. I don't think any one is likely to run across us in this out-of-the-way place."

"I don't think so, either," responded Hiram, and was soon asleep and snoring.

The breakfast programme of the previous morning was repeated later.

Hiram called the whole thing a picnic, and was jolly and happy.

"One thing, though," he said; "isn't something exciting going to happen soon, Dave?"

"We ought to be pretty well satisfied with the splendid cruise of the Monarch II," suggested Dave.

"Yes, but I'm getting anxious to run across some of the smugglers. I've read a lot about them in the papers and books. They must be great fellows to tackle, with their cutlasses, and walking the plank, and treasure hoards."

"Why, Hiram," laughed Dave, "you're not thinking of smugglers."

"What am I then?"

"Pirates."

"Oh, yes, that's so," agreed Hiram. "Well, the Dawsons are worse than pirates. They won't give up that airship without a tussle, I can tell you."

"All I want to do is to locate them," said Dave. "The government will do the rest."

Dave left the camp, as they called it, about noon. He had some difficulty in getting from the island to the mainland, as the soil was soggy and at places two feet deep with water. He accomplished the task, however, with only a slight wetting.

The young aviator had been given the address, of one of Mr. Price's men at Ironton. He visited his office, but found him absent for the day. Then he wired his progress to the Interstate people and told them if necessary to reach, him at the Northern Hotel.

Dave went to the hotel and made arrangement with the clerk as to mail and telegrams. He decided to remain in the vicinity of Ironton till he got in touch with the revenue officer's agent there. He was just leaving the hotel when one placed a hand on his shoulder, with the friendly words:

"Why, hello, Dashaway."

Dave turned quickly, startled for a moment. Then his face broke into smiles of warm welcome.

"Mr. Alden," he said, and returned the friendly hand clasp of his companion.

The chance meeting took Dave's mind back instantly to a most pleasant period of his experience since leaving his guardian's home at Brookville.

It was Mr. Alden, the moving picture man, who had given Dave what might be called his first start in business life. Dave had posed for the "movies," and later he and Mr. King had taken a prominent part in some motion pictures bringing in the monoplane, the Aegis.

"I didn't expect to see you way up here, Dashaway," spoke Mr. Alden.

"How are you getting along?"

"First class, thanks to the friendly help you gave me in the first place," responded the young aviator.

"I'm glad of that. Come up to my room and tell me all about it, Dashaway. Now then, for a talk over old times," resumed the moving picture man, as they were comfortably seated in his room at the hotel.

Dave parried a good many questions. He did not exactly wish to tell Mr. Alden about his business, which in the present case was also that of his employers. He managed to lead Mr. Alden to talk of his own affairs.

"Oh, I've had the actors up here on a lot of marine scenarios," explained the moving picture man. "They went away only this morning. We've been picturing 'The Island Hermit of Lake Superior,' 'Iron Miners' Revenge,' 'Flight Across the Border,' and 'The Mystery of the Pineries.' Great scenery around here for fittings, you see. There are some of my key negatives on the table there, look them over."

Dave examined some of the films with interest. The former kindness of Mr. Alden and his party had left a warm spot in the heart of the young aviator for anything concerning the movies.

"There's some plain slides we made to catch the costumes and figures," added Mr. Alden, pointing to a rack containing about a dozen glass negatives.

Dave began holding them up to the light in turn. He had inspected perhaps one half of them, when he somewhat startled the moving picture man with a sharp sudden exclamation.

"Mr. Alden," he asked quite excitedly, "where did you take that slide?"

CHAPTER XVIII

ON DESERT ISLAND

The young aviator might well ask the question he put to the moving picture man, for the negative in Dave's hand showed plainly the face and figure of Jerry Dawson.

There could be no mistake. The boy who had run away with the Drifter had features strongly marked and not readily forgotten. The picture had been taken in the open street. Jerry was standing there talking to a Chinaman.

"Some scene you know, Dashaway?" asked Mr. Alden.

"No, somebody I know—and am very anxious to find," replied Dave.

"So? Let me have a look at it."

Dave handed the plate to the moving picture man, who slanted it against the light and nodded intelligently.

"Oh, that?" he said. "Yes, I remember all about it."

"Where did you take it, Mr. Alden?" pressed Dave.

"At Anseton. There's a sort of foreign quarter there, and I was catching up some street scenes. It was the Chinaman I shot. Wanted the costume, you know."

"When was that?" asked Dave.

"Yesterday morning."

Dave asked a score of questions. The moving picture man saw that Dave had some important motive in his inquiries. He did not ask what it was, and was patient and careful in his replies.

Dave left Mr. Alden feeling that he had learned a good deal. The presence of Jerry Dawson in Anseton, and that, too, with a Chinaman, verified many of the theories of the young aviator. Dave lost no time in getting to a telegraph office, to send a dispatch that would reach Mr. Price. It told briefly of the progress of the Monarch II and of the definite clew Dave had just discovered.

That afternoon our hero hired a hand cart he saw in a blacksmith's yard labeled "For Sale." He drove it as near to the swamp island as he could, without getting stuck in the mud. Then, he called to Hiram, who put himself in wading trim. The empty gasoline cans were over to the cart by Hiram. Dave trundled them to the town, got them filled and to the island, and, returning the cart, was ready to prepare for a new night journey.

"It's less than sixty miles that we have to go, Hiram," he advised his assistant.

"Then you've found out something definite?" guessed Hiram.

"Yes, I have got a trace of Jerry Dawson."

"You don't say so!"

"I do, and I'll tell you how," and Dave recited the story of his meeting with the moving picture man.

"Why, that's just grand," commented Hiram in his exuberant way.

"You've good as run down the Drifter."

"Not quite, Hiram."

"Oh, you'll find the stolen airship. I feel it in my bones. I've felt it ever since I saw the way you took hold of this affair."

"Well, I've had good help and a splendid machine, you must remember."

"I don't go much on the help," declared Hiram modestly. "As to the Monarch II, though, I never saw such a well-behaved machine. If she does in the water what she's done in the air, she's a record breaker, sure."

The machine was put in the best possible trim. It lacked two hours of nightfall but Dave had plenty to occupy his mind. For over an hour he sat looking over maps and memoranda, and blocking out his course. He had been very explicit and painstaking in questioning the moving picture man. He had made inquiries concerning Anseton and its vicinity down to the smallest detail. From all this Dave had decided on a permanent landing place, a sort of headquarters from which he could branch out in his personal investigations in the day time and sally forth on an air hunt in the dark.

The aviators could distinctly hear a bell in some tower tolling the hour of nine as they circled a busy city that lay beyond and below, them, a blur of light. Dave at the levers kept the Monarch II at a fair height, constantly scanning an expanse to the north dotted only here and there with lights. Once past the outskirts of the city he turned due north.

"Why, hello!" exclaimed his companion, "we're over water!"

"Yes," replied Dave, "it's the lake."

"Lake Superior! Dave, are we going to cross it?"

"A good many times in the future probably, but not tonight. I am looking for a revolving light west of the city, right along the coast."

"I'll keep a lookout, too."

The lake was here and there dotted with the signal lights of steamers. Along the shore, which Dave skirted closely, various lights their met view. Both boys strained their gaze. Finally Hiram called out sharply: "I see it, Dave."

"See what?"

"A revolving light."

"Where?"

"See, just beyond that little cluster of town lights—quite high up."

"Yes," answered Dave in a tone of satisfaction. "That is Rocky

Point lighthouse. I know my bearings, now."

"Are you going to land, Dave?"

"Presently."

"But you're driving out further over the lake."

"Just for a short distance, Hiram," advised Dave. "There's an island down shore where they run a smelter—ah, I think I locate it."

Dave was not mistaken. He came within range of some tall, stacks sending out sparks and flames. Now he changed his course. He kept his glance fixed below him and to the right as steadily as his duties at the lever would permit.

The Monarch II passed over two small islands. Half a mile beyond them arose a third larger one. It was quite prominent, for the reason, that it presented a range of great cliffs. Dave navigated the air in narrowing circles. Then, timing and calculating a volplane glide, he let the machine down easily to the ground.

"Well!" ejaculated Hiram, "you've hit on a pretty dark spot for a camp, Dave."

"And a safe one," replied the young aviator. "Mr. Alden described this place to me. It is called Desert Island, and has no inhabitants on it. It seems dark because we are so shut in, but your eyes will soon become used to that."

It was a singular place into which the Monarch II had descended.

High declivitous, masses of rock formed a sort of immense cairn.

They seemed shut in on every side, fully one hundred feet below the

level of the cliffs.

The farther north they had run the cooler air currents had become.

Both boys felt somewhat chilly.

"See here," spoke Hiram, after they had seen that the machine was all right and a rubber sheet thrown over the machinery to protect it from the heavy night dews, "a warm cup coffee wouldn't hurt us."

"That's right, Hiram," agreed Dave. "We are all shut in here, and even a big fire wouldn't show from the land or the deck of a passenger steamer. You can try your hand at coffee making, if you like."

"The coffee is all made, but cold, in these bottles," explained

Hiram, fishing out two from the accommodation basket.

There were both trees and bushes near by. Hiram gathered some dry branches and roots and soon had a comfortable little campfire going. He poured out the coffee from the bottles into a tin water pail, and soon had it steaming hot. Sandwiches and some bakery stuff Dave had bought at Ironton made a very satisfactory meal. Then they spread some wraps over a heap of dried grass, which they gathered up without much trouble. They rested in luxurious ease, watching the bright, snapping fire glow and feeling its genial warmth.

"Well, this is just like Robinson Crusoe, isn't it, Dave?" asked

Hiram, with an air of great comfort.

"If you are a man Friday, then," rejoined the young aviator with a smile, "you scout around in the morning and see if there are any breaks in these great walls of rock shutting us in."

"Oh, then you're not counting an leaving here again by the air route?" inquired Hiram in some surprise.

"Not in daylight. I want to find some other way out for that. You see," explained Dave, "this is just an ideal spot as a rendezvous. I want to get over to the city tomorrow, though, to attend to some important business."

"How are you going to get there?"

"Why, I'll have to trust to my swimming skill, I guess," replied

Dave.

"Um-m," observed Hiram thoughtfully, and, if the young aviator had been more watchful, he would have noticed that for the rest of the evening his willing assistant seemed to have something on his mind.

CHAPTER XIX

THE SEARCHLIGHT

"Hallo! Hallo!"

Dave made the echoes ring with the loud call as he moved up and down and across the queer basin, or cairn, where they had landed in the Monarch II the night previous.

He had awakened just at daylight to find Hiram Dobbs mysteriously missing. Dave was not worried at the first, but as he looked around and then explored the immediate neighborhood, he began to get mystified, if not alarmed.

Neither did his vigorous shouting bring any response. Dave came back to the camp spot to make a new discovery that puzzled him. On the ground near where they had slept were Hiram's coat, vest, shoes and cap.

"Why, I can't understand this at all," mused the young aviator. "Hiram couldn't have done much in the way of climbing up, he appears to be nowhere within hail, and he is not given to play tricks."

Dave did not wait to eat anything. He was really concerned about his comrade. He got a long tree branch, stripped it, and went along the side of the cairn, poking in and out among the dense dumps of shrubbery.

"Hello," he exclaimed suddenly, as disturbing some vines he saw an opening, and not twenty feet away a natural rocky tunnel, "daylight, and the waves of the lake. I think I understand now."

Dave penetrated the passage. As he came out at the other end, he found he faced a rock-strewn stretch of sand. The waves of the lake lapped this. In the distance he could make out Anseton, and nearer still, about a mile distant, the main shore.

The shore he was on terminated in a ridge of rocks that ran far out into the water. Dave wondered if the exploring spirit had moved Hiram to attempt an entire circle about the island.

"He went away in swimming trim," thought Dave, "so that may be so.

I'll go out on that ledge of rocks and explore a little myself."

"Hello, Dave Dashaway!" sang out an exultant voice, just as Dave was about to remove his shoes.

Around the ledge of rock came a light skiff. The oarsman was Dave's missing comrade. He drove the boat upon the sandy beach and leaped out with a gay laugh.

"Why, Hiram," exclaimed the young aviator in marked surprise.

"It's me," chuckled Hiram. "Stole a march on you. Nearly dry," he added, shaking his clinging garments. "And oh! what a swim."

"You have been to the mainland?" questioned Dave.

"Where else? When you said 'swim' last night, it gave me an idea. I'm some swimmer, Dave Dashaway. Always was. Took the prize in a contest in Plum Creek back at home one Fourth of July. I found a way out of that shut in place and made a jolly dive for shore."

"But the skiff?"

"You'll need one, won't you?" challenged Hiram.

"Why, yes. I intended hiring one when I got across from the island."

"So you said, and I acted. I did better than hiring a boat, Dave."

"How is that?"

"Bought one outright. I took my money with me. Found an old fellow who lets out a lot of boats for fishing, and made a bargain. The skiff isn't the staunchest craft on the lake. Leaks a little, and one oar has been split and mended, but it's all right for our little use. Four dollars and a half—and we can sell it for something when we get through using it."

"You're a great fellow, Hiram, I must confess," said Dave admiringly.

"I'd like to do something to help on this trip of ours, you know."

"You've done a good deal this time, I can tell you that," declared

Dave. "I can manage all my plans finely, now."

They pulled the boat into the shelter of some rocks. Then they returned to the rocky hollow. A good breakfast was in order. Dave announced the importance of his getting to Anseton at once.

An hour later the little skiff was launched once more. Dave rowed over to the mainland and lined the shore till well into city waters. He secured the skiff near a public pier, and started on foot for his destination.

Left to himself on the island, Hiram proceeded to dry his clothing. Then he puttered about the machine. He read for an hour or two in a book on aeronautics he found in the basket, well on towards the afternoon.

Hiram got tired of waiting for Dave. He went through the tunnel finally and roamed about on the rocky shore. There was more of scenery and variety here. The youth watched the boats in the distance. Then he made out the little skiff he had bought that morning making its way in and out among other craft between the island, and the mainland.

"What's the news, Dave?" inquired Hiram, as they gained the camp after securing the skiff where it could not be easily seen or found.

"The best ever," reported Dave cheerily.

"Tell me about it, won't you?"

"Well, I saw Mr. Price."

"Is he here at Anseton?"

"Yes, with his men. I had a long talk with him. He feels pretty good to know that we got here safely with the Monarch II. I told him all about the place where the moving picture man saw Jerry Dawson and the Chinaman. He thinks that is an excellent clew."

"I should think it was," said Hiram.

"He wants us to try and discover the Drifter. He says it's only a question of time, he and his men running down the smugglers. You see, Hiram, we are interested mainly in finding the aero-hydroplane, and getting it back to the Interstate people."

"That's so."

"And we must think of that first."

"I understand."

"We will make a long trip tonight—clear across the lake."

"Suppose you get a sight of the Drifter?"

"Then we'll know that it is really here, won't we?"

"Yes, but are you going to jog right into them and capture them?"

"Hardly," laughed Dave. "I hope if we do come across the Drifter, that we can follow it or keep it company, or find out where it is hidden away in the daytime. We will have to run across it before we can decide what circumstances will lead us to do."

"They're an ugly crowd—the Dawsons, and probably the fellows with them, too."

"I realize that. Mr. Price insisted on my taking these," and Dave began opening a boxlike package he had brought with him in the skiff.

"Hello," cried Hiram, as two good sized weapons and some boxes of cartridges were disclosed. "Do we have to use them?"

"I hope not," replied Dave, "but Mr. Price said we might come to a pinch where we could use them to show we were not unprotected, and to scare any crowd that tried to interfere with us."

"Well, it begins to look like real business," commented Hiram.

"That's what we're here for."

"Yes, indeed."

They had no difficulty in getting the Monarch II aloft, the hollow extending for several hundred feet. The night was ideal for a secret sky voyage. A slight mist hung over the ground, but at a height of five hundred feet the air was perfectly clear. There was bright starlight, and against the radiance they could make out flying birds quite a distance away.

Dave took a route across the lake diagonally from Anseton. They skirted the other shore for about ten miles. Then they recrossed the lake. The machine made a sweep along the coast line.

"Well, Dave," remarked his trusty assistant, "we've run across no air bird so far."

"I didn't expect to, all at once," was Dave's reply. "We can only keep at it."

"And trust to luck—I say!"

Hiram interrupted himself with a shout. Just beneath them an excursion steamer was ploughing its way through the waves, bound citywards on its return trip. They could hear the music of the band aboard, until now drowned out by hoarse blare of the fog whistle.

At the same moment a broad vivid flare of electric radiance shot across the sky from the deck of the steamer. It waved horizontally in some signal to the landing dock two miles further away. Then the operator of this glowing searchlight sent its gleams upwards in a slow way, as if for scenic effect for the passengers on board.

"The mischief!" exclaimed Dave bending to levers and starting the

Monarch II forward at best speed.

Hiram sat staring. He blinked, half-blinded. The machine was irradiated in clear, sharp outlines as the great searchlight glare was focused, a speck of action in the sky.

A chorus of cheers went up from the deck of the steamer as its passengers caught sight of the airship. Only for a moment, however, was the brilliant sky picture in view. Dave turned the head of the machine on a volplane sweep, and the searchlight operator could not locate it again.

"Well, we've been seen," observed Hiram,

"I'm sorry for it," replied Dave simply.

"Look there!" cried Hiram abruptly.

Dave had selected a course leading over the land, away from the water. As Hiram spoke, his own eye caught sight of some brilliant sparkles of light.

It was a rocket, exploding in mid air directly in their course, and it was to this that Hiram Dobbs had directed the attention of the young aviator.

CHAPTER XX

ACROSS THE BORDER

"Did you see it?" asked Hiram, in a great state of excitement.

"Yes," responded Dave. "A rocket."

"See! See!" continued Hiram-"there's it second one!"

"Sure enough."

"Dave, this means something."

"For us, you think?"

"Yes, I do. Keep near the place where these rockets were fired,

Dave. Now then, what do you think?"

Dave slowed down. There was certainly something to his companion's surmises or suspicions, whatever they were. Directly at the spot whence the rockets had been fired there now suddenly flared up a great reach of flames.

Watching these, the interested aviators saw them change to a reddish hue. Three times, at brief intervals, they did this.

"Don't you see?" persisted Hiram.

"See what?" asked Dave.

"A signal."

"You think so?"

"I surely do. Now, then, look sharp. There are figures about the fire. The fire is pitch or oil, or something that could be made to flame up quickly. One of the men threw something into it from a box. It was red fire."

"Why, yes," observed Dave slowly. "I'll admit that was some kind of a signal."

"For the airship," interrupted Hiram quickly. "Look, look again, Dave! One of the men is shading his eyes from the glare of the fire, and is looking straight up into the sky. Why, it's plain as day. They saw our airship when that searchlight caught us. They were waiting for an airship to come along."

"Another airship than ours, you mean?"

"That's it, and I'll bet the Drifter! They took ours for the Drifter. They want us to land. Why, see there, one of the fellows is looking through a field glass—as if he could make us out in the dark away up here!"

It did not take Dave long to drift to Hiram's way of thinking. The spot where the fire showed seemed to be a large yard of some kind, attached to a factory.

"Of course this is all guess work, Hiram," said Dave, after a moment's thought. "Just the same, it fits in to your theory."

"Say," spoke Hiram suddenly, "I've an idea."

"What is it, Hiram?"

"Make a stop just as soon as you can."

"What's that for?"

"Let me out, and give me a chance to find out who that signal was intended for."

"I declare, it's not a bad plan," said Dave at once.

"Can't you find some safe place where we can land?"

"There won't be much trouble about that."

"Do it, Dave," urged Hiram, "and right away, so I won't lose track of the place yonder."

Dave inspected the country below as closely as he could at a distance. He circled to a lower level, and selected a patch of high grass between two corn fields.

"Now then," announced Hiram. "I'm off."

"I shall wait anxiously for your return, Hiram."

"Don't worry, I shan't get into any trouble."

Dave did not leave the flying machine. He kept himself in readiness for a flight, should anyone approach the spot. There was not much fear of that, though, he reasoned, as the place was away from the traversed roads and paths.

The young aviator had quite a spell of waiting. He began to fear that Hiram had lost his way or that something had happened to him, as an hour passed by. Suddenly, however, his active young assistant bounded into view, chipper and lively as usual.

"What news, Hiram?" inquired Dave.

"The best in the world."

"You have found out something?"

"You'll think so when I tell you," declared Hiram. "I found the place where they sent up the rockets without much trouble."

"What was it, Hiram?"

"An old factory yard. Part of the buildings have been burned down, and three or four loaferish looking fellows seem to live in an old shake down there. They belong to the crowd of that fellow, Ridgely, the smuggler, right enough."

"How did you know that, Hiram?" asked Dave.

"Because I overheard them. They had let their signal fire burn down low, and were sitting around it talking. I crept up behind an old shed and listened. It was as near as I dared to get, and I could catch only a word now and then. They spoke the name Drifter," asserted Hiram positively.

"You didn't see anything of Jerry Dawson?" asked Dave.

"No, but—say, yes, they mentioned his name, too. They were all excited about seeing our airship. It seems they were trying to warn the Drifter."

"To warn the Drifter?" repeated Dave somewhat puzzled.

"Yes."

"Why, what for?"

"To keep away from the American shore. Somehow, they had found out that the revenue officers were at Anseton. They knew, too, that the Interstate people had an airship out after them. It seems that when we didn't reply to their signal, they guessed that they had hailed the wrong airship. They have sent a man to the city to telegraph to the men on the Canadian side to look out for an airship on their track."

"You don't know where they are going to telegraph to, Hiram?"

"But I do," cried Hiram triumphantly. "That's my big discovery. They talked over the whole thing. The message is to be sent to a friend at Brantford. He is to ride post haste horseback ten miles west of that place to where the Drifter people have a camp in what they call Big Moose Woods."

"Hiram," applauded the young aviator, "you're a jewel. Why, you have simplified the whole business."

"And you're going right after the Drifter?" propounded Hiram eagerly.

"'We're going to try to," replied Dave, "but first we must get word of all this to Mr. Price."

The Monarch II had mounted aloft while they were conversing. Dave started the machine in a direction opposite to that in which they had been going. Hiram noted this.

"Are you going back to Desert Island?" he asked.

"First, yes. Then I shall skiff over to Anseton and report to Mr.

Price direct or through any of his agents I may find."

The machine was brought safely to her old moorings within an hour. Dave, after landing on Desert Island, at once rowed over to the mainland. Hiram was full of curiosity when he returned.

"It's all right," Dave explained. "I was lucky enough to meet Mr. Price himself. He and his men had already acted on the clew that picture of Jerry and the Chinaman gave us. The old factory yard where the rockets were sent up will be under watch before the night is over, and Mr. Price is going to Brantford on a special boat."

"Then the crowd who stole the Drifter are as good as caught!" exclaimed Hiram hopefully.

"Hardly," replied Dave. "Mr. Price has advised me to get the

Monarch II over to the Canadian side of the lake to night!"

"Which you are going to do, Dave?"

"Right away."

Dave, while in Anseton, had made some necessary inquiries as to the location of Brantford. He had also got a very good idea of Big Moose Woods. His arrangements with the revenue officer had been precise. He was aware that their only chance of getting near to the missing airship was to make new headquarters somewhere in the vicinity of Brantford, just as they had on Desert Island.

The darkness was fading in the east when Dave selected a plateau on the top of a high hill as a landing place. Once landed, trees and bushes at its crest hid them from view except from overhead. Dave had used diligence and haste in getting out of possible sight, for day was breaking.

They had reach Brantford, sailed over it, and Dave calculated had skirted the vicinity of Big Moose Woods. Nowhere, however, had lights, a campfire or any other token indicated the camp or rendezvous of the Drifter party.

"We are within twenty miles of Brantford," Dave announced.

"And what's the programme?" inquired Hiram.

"Sleep, for we need it. We seem to be safely shut in here. Later we'll plan just what we will do."

"If the Dawson crowd are warned all around about us and the revenue officers, they may run for some other territory," suggested Hiram.

"We want to be on the lookout for that," replied the young aviator.

They made themselves a comfortable bed, and both were soon asleep. Hiram woke up first; and found the sun shining in his eyes, and was about to shift his position, intent on a longer nap, when he checked himself not moving a muscle.

Through his half closed eyelids, still feigning sleep, Hiram kept his glance fixed on one spot. He almost held his breath. Thus for nearly five minutes he lay inert, but every nerve on the keenest edge.

His glance widened and seemed to be following some disappearing object. Then he sat straight upright, stared fixedly down the hill, and leaning over pulled his companion by the sleeve.

"Dave! Dave!" whispered the excited boy-"wake up! We've been discovered!"

CHAPTER XXI

A CHASE IN MID AIR

Dave roused up, wide awake in an instant. He was about to spring to his feet, when Hiram pulled him back with the words:

"Don't get up."

"Why not?" inquired the somewhat puzzled young aviator.

"You'll be seen."

"Who by?"

"A man who was just here."

"Do you mean that, Hiram?" exclaimed Dave in a startled tone.

"I certainly do. Look," said Hiram, pointing, and then he added: "No, the trees shut him out now. As I just said, though, we have been discovered."

Now Hiram arose to his feet, the danger of being seen appearing to have passed. Dave followed his example.

"Some one was here, you say?" began Dave.

"Yes."

"Who was it?"

"A fellow who looked like some of the half breed Indians we saw fishing over near Anseton. I woke up, and he came in range clear as a picture. It was over by that thicket of pine trees. There he stood, staring at our machine, then at us. He seemed to take it in with a good deal of surprise. Finally he threw up his hands as if he was making up his mind to something, and started on a run down the hill."

"In that direction?" asked Dave, pointing due east.

"Yes, in the direction of Brantford. I tell you, Dave, he's a spy. If he ran across us accidentally then he's gone to tell his friends about discovering the airship."

"That doesn't follow," remarked Dave thoughtfully, "but I'm glad you saw him."

"Yes, I think we need to keep a pretty close lookout. Say, Dave," questioned Hiram, "if he is some friend of the Dawson crowd, and has gone to tell them about us, what do you suppose they'll do?"

"I have no idea," replied the young aviator. "But they won't catch us napping."

Dave kept a close watch out in all directions while Hiram hurried up a quick breakfast. They got through with the meal rapidly. Then Dave went over the machine, seeing that the gasoline tanks were full and the gearing and oiling apparatus in good order.

Two hours went by, and there were no developments that indicated that the visitor to their camp had been other than a straggler, with no purpose in view in his rapid disappearance. Hiram became more matter-of-fact, and guessed he had "got scared for nothing." All the same he kept a close lookout all of the time, particularly in the direction of Brantford.

Dave was planning a visit on foot to that town. He decided, however, that he would wait till afternoon so as to be sure that there was no occasion for worry. Both lads discovered the fallacy of their theories at the same moment.

"Look!" suddenly shouted Hiram, pointing.

"I see," said Dave calmly, but under the surface greatly stirred up.

"It's the Drifter!"

"Yes."

"What are you going to do?"

"Come," spoke Dave simply, and sprang into his seat in the Machine.

Hiram hastily collected their few belongings scattered about the spot. He bundled them into the accommodation basket, and was in his place almost as soon as Dave.

The eyes of both of the young aviators were fixed on a rapidly approaching object—an airship. Dave did not have to glance at its construction more than once to know definitely that it was the stolen Drifter.

Whoever was at the levers, Jerry or his father, thoroughly understood his business, Dave saw that. The aero-hydroplane came rather abruptly into view over a wooded hill top, and was rapidly approaching them.

"You see, I was right," said Hiram hastily. "That half breed was a spy, at least to that crowd. He has directed them here."

"All ready," ordered Dave, in a set, sturdy tone, and the self starter began to work.

"What is it—a chase?" fluttered Hiram.

"We'll have to wait and see. You know what kind of fellows the Dawsons are. I'm not going to sit like a bird in a nest and have them swoop down upon us, though."

"There are three—you can count them in their airship," said Hiram, shading his eyes and craning his neck.

"Four," corrected Dave. "The Drifter has a capacity of five ordinary people, Mr. Randolph told me."

The Monarch II made a magnificent slanting rise up into the air. Dave knew the splendid qualities of the machine under his control. They included an ability for a quick light ascent. He had no idea of the purpose of the Drifter crowd, but of course their main object was to capture their rival. The question was, failing in this, how, far would they go in the way of crippling or even destroying the Monarch II.

The Drifter was headed on a course directly towards the eminence which the boys had just left behind them. There had come up an eight hour wind about noon, and Dave knew that would be child's play maneuvering to avoid the enemy intent on annoying or injuring them. He drove ahead at a six hundred feet level and waited for the Drifter crowd to indicate what their purpose was.

"They are changing their course!" said Hiram quickly, as the Drifter wheeled suddenly.

"They are going to try a new ascent," explained Dave.

"Why?"

"To get to a higher level than ourselves."

"Then they mean mischief?"

"I am afraid that they do," replied the young aviator.

"Maybe they are trying to scare us," suggested Hiram.

Dave was now certain that the purpose of the Dawsons was to pursue, capture or intimidate them, or drive them away. They had a superb machine, and as they made a far lateral shoot it brought them considerably higher up than the Monarch II.

In fact, after one or two circles, like a huge bird swooping after prey, the Drifter came almost directly over them.

Dave's tactics were now purely defensive and evasive. There were five people aboard the aero-hydroplane, and they were desperate persons. He was not surprised when an object same shooting downwards from the Drifter. It struck one of the plane wires and then dropped earthwards.

"Something's whipped loose," spoke Hiram quickly.

"It's one of the elevator wires," said Dave, darting a quick glance at the spot. "This won't do."

Now it was an over-water flight with no measured course to pursue. The Drifter tried to repeat its recent tactics. Dave noticed that the Monarch II had become somewhat faulty in its running. He was anxious to get away from the enemy. His main efforts were directed towards preserving a sure balance, for once or twice there was a wobble, as if the machine was hurt in some vital part.

The young aviator made out a buoy a few miles to the west. Beyond it was a little settlement. He set his course for reaching it, and directed his full attention to the levers and the angle indicated.

The indicator was directly in front of the pilot seat. It showed positively how the machine was flying, on the top or down bank. It comprised a cup with lines set about ten degrees, and gave a sure safety limit. Only the pendulum was movable. This was mounted on an arm always perpendicular, a small mirror reflecting the variations of the pendulum.

Climbing and banking, Dave got quite a lead on the Drifter, but the aero-hydroplane kept up a steady pursuit.

"There's something the matter besides the broken wire," spoke Dave to his anxious companion. "The oil intake is dogged or one of the planes loose. We can't take any risks."

Dave sent the Monarch II on a downward shoot. There was a single pontoon in the center of the craft, with small tanks beneath the planes to prevent tipping over in the water. Dave aimed to hit the bay near to the shore.

Suddenly the aircraft acted queer. It had evidently struck a hole in the air. The machine seemed fairly to drop from under its occupants, and thirty feet from the water, Dave was lifted from his seat and took a sudden plunge over-board.

He went under the surface and came up dazed and nearly stunned. As he floated, dashing the water from his eyes, he saw the Drifter, now a flying boat, cut around a point of rocks, bearing straight down upon him.

Dave looked quickly about him for the Monarch II. To his surprise, as it scudded across the waves for perhaps a hundred feet on its momentum, it lifted again free of the surface of the bay.

He made out Hiram clambering from his seat like a sailor among the riggings of a ship. He saw the machine go up on a sharp slant, clear the shore of the bay, and disappear beyond the high cliffs lining it.

Then something struck him. It was some light part of the rotary engined aero-hydroplane, the Drifter, cutting the water like a knife. His head dizzied, and the young aviator went under the surface of the lake with a shock.

CHAPTER XXII

DAVE A CAPTIVE

It took Dave an hour to find out just what had happened to him. He roused up to find two men carrying him, one at his feet, one at his shoulders. All that he could guess was that they were on land. How he had been fished out of the water, and what had become of the Drifter, the young aviator had no means of knowing.

The two men were rough looking fellows and reminded Dave of dock laborers or loiterers. They were big and sturdy, and as Dave stretched out and showed signs of life, one of them remarked gruffly.

"None of that—no squirming, now."

Dave's clothes were soggy and dripping. He felt somewhat sore on one side of his head, but so far as he could figure it out he was not crippled; or seriously hurt.

The young aviator cast his eyes about him to, learn that they were going through a patch of timber. Then came a meadow-like stretch, and then a thicket. They had not gone far into that before the men dropped him on the ground and stood over him.

"Can you walk?" asked one of the two.

"I think I can," replied Dave, arising quite nimbly to his feet.

The instant he did this both of the men reached, out and seized an arm. Dave was thus pinioned tightly as the men forced him along.

"Most there," growled one of them gruffly.

"Good thing," retorted the other.

Finally they came to a dense thicket that covered a rise. About half way up this, almost hidden by saplings and vines, Dave made out a grim looking patched-up building.

It was an old hut to which various additions had been made. One of Dave's companions uttered a peculiar whistle. The door of the place was opened, and a disreputable looking fellow like themselves admitted them.

"Hello, who's this?" he spoke in a tone of curiosity.

"Oh, some one to take care of," was the short reply.

"He don't look like a revenue."

"Worse than that. Ridgely will tell you when he comes," was the indifferent retort. "Have you a place to keep him tight and safe?"

"I guess so," laughed the other, "a dozen of them."

"One will do."

Dave was led through several rooms. Then they came to a partition formed of heavy timbers. In its center was a stout door with an immense padlock.

"Get in there," spoke the most ferocious of his captors, giving Dave a push.

Then the door was closed with a crash that showed how heavy it was.

Dave could hear those outside securing the padlock.

"A prisoner, eh?" mused Dave, looking about him. "Yes, it is, indeed, tight and safe."

Dave's prison place was gruesome in the extreme. On three sides was solid rock, forming a semicircular back to the room. The partition, closed the entire front. Near its top in several places were cut out apertures, admitting air and a little light.

There were some broken boxes in the place and a heap of burlap. Dave decided that it had been used at some time or other as a place of storage. He did not yet feel normal, so he sat down on one of the boxes and felt about his head.

"Just a bruise," he reported. "I suppose they, dragged me aboard of the Drifter from the water, but what about Hiram and the Monarch II?"

Dave started up, all weakness and dizziness disappearing as if by magic, as he thrilled over the possible peril of his comrade. With a recollection only of his last sight of Hiram grid the Monarch II, he feared what might have happened to either or both.

It worried Dave a good deal and made him restless and unhappy, but finally he figured out a theory. In some unaccountable way the Monarch II had no sooner glided along on its pontoon, than it had run straightway up into the air, as though the self starter was in perfect action. Dave recalled Hiram struggling to reach the pilot's seat. Then he had witnessed the disappearance of the Monarch II.

"I doubt if Hiram could manage the machine—I even doubt with something wrong with it, as there surely was, if he could keep it adrift," decided Dave. "What then?"

The young aviator pictured Hiram and the machine in a tangle among the trees, or dropping upset among the rocks. He had not seen anything of the Dawsons or the Drifter since he had fallen into the water of the bay. Perhaps, he reasoned, they had resumed an air chase of the fugitive.

Dave had several hours to himself. He detected no sound or movement outside of the strange room he was in. It was dreadfully dull and lonesome, and he wondered what the outcome of his present adventure would be.

It was well along in the day, when Dave from sheer weariness and worry had lain down among the heaps of burlap, that a diversion came to monotony. He started up as he heard voice outside of the door. Then the padlock rattled, the door opened, and some one stepped across the threshold. The visitor stared about to locate Dave, and spoke the words:

"That you, Dashaway?"

The room was lighter now, with the door half open. Dave rubbed his eyes and strained his gaze, and took a good look at the speaker.

"Don't you know me?" challenged the latter.

"Oh, yes," replied Dave, "I see now. You are the gentleman we rescued from the lake at Columbus."

"I don't suppose you think me much of a gentleman just now,

Dashaway," spoke Ridgely, for, he was, in fact Dave's visitor.

His tone was somewhat regretful, and not at all unfriendly. Dave was shrewd enough to discover this, and politic enough to take quick advantage of it.

"Oh, I don't know," he said. "Of course you are with the crowd who had me locked in here."

"I'm sorry to say that's true," responded Ridgely.

"It's not pleasant here, I can tell you," said Dave, "and the whole thing is pretty high handed, don't you think so, Mr. Ridgely?"

"I don't think it, Dashaway, I know, it. See here, I've got nothing against you. On the contrary, I owe you a good deal. I'm not forgetting that you saved my life when my launch struck the rocks near Columbus."

Dave was silent, resolved to let the man have his say out.

"I was in a fix then, I was in a fix before I got there, and I'm afraid I'm in a fix now," continued Ridgely. "I've come to see you in the right spirit, Dashaway."

"How is that?" inquired Dave.

"Sick of the whole combination. I thought I was smart, but you and your people are smarter. Young Dawson convinced me that we could run things so our airship could make trips for a long time, and here you are on our trail within seventy-two hours."

"Yes, Mr. Ridgely," acknowledged the young aviator. "They found a clew and started pursuit right after you stole the Drifter."

"You mean you did. Don't be modest, Dashaway. I've learned a good deal about you, and if I hadn't about decided to quit business I'd offer you a job."

"What!" smiled Dave—"smuggling?"

"Well, it pays pretty big, you know."

"Does it?" replied Dave. "I fail to see it. I wouldn't like to be in a position where I was being chased half over the country."

"H'm, we won't discuss it," retorted Ridgely in a moody tone. "I came to tell you that you won't be hurt any."

"But I want to get away from here," insisted Dave.

"That will be all, too," Ridgely assured him. "You see, we know now that things are going to break up. I don't suppose you would tell me how closely the revenue officers are on our track."

"So close," replied Dave gravely, "that you won't dare to cross the border any more."

"Are they on the Canadian side yet?" questioned Ridgely anxiously.

"I don't know that, and I shouldn't feel right in telling you if I did," replied Dave. "You had better let me go, Mr. Ridgely. It won't sound well, when things get righted, that you kept me a prisoner here."

"I haven't all the say about that, Dashaway," confessed Ridgely in a rueful way. "I don't think the Dawsons will let you go until they are sure of making themselves safe."

"Do you know what became of our airship, Mr. Ridgely?" Dave asked pointedly.

"No, I don't—none of us do. Young Dawson is pretty good in the air, but he didn't seem to know how to get off the water quickly. After we got you aboard, we lost a lot of time getting you ashore, and, up in the air again, when we started in the direction we had seen your airship go, we could find no trace of it."

"I hope nothing his happened to Hiram," thought Dave, very anxiously.

"If I get away," resumed Ridgely, "I want you to tell the people after me, if you can, that I'm all through with the smuggling business. I've had my fill of it."

The speaker turned to leave the room, but Dave halted him with the question:

"What are you going to do about me, Mr. Ridgely?"

"I am going to order the people here to treat you the best they know how," was the prompt response.

"That's all very well enough," said Dave, "but I have business to attend to."

"What business, Dashaway?"

"Our airship and my friend."

Ridgely looked troubled. He was thoughtfully, silent for a moment or two. Then he said:

"Look here, Dashaway, our men are looking for your airship, and that means your friend, too, of course. I've got to go to Brantford, but I shall leave word that they must look after your friend, and let you go the minute I send back word that the coast is clear for them to scatter."

"But what about the Drifter, Mr. Ridgley?" persisted Dave. "It is the property of my employers. I came after it, and I want it."

A faint smile of mingled amusement and admiration crossed the face of Ridgely. Reckless fellow that he was, he could not fail to recognize the fact that Dave, indeed, had business to attend to.

"You take it pretty cool, Dashaway," he observed.

"Because I am in the right," asserted Dave, "as you well know. The Dawsons are malicious people. I want you to warn them that if they do, any unnecessary injury to the Drifter, it will make it the worse for them in the final reckoning that is bound to come."

"I don't think they will do the airship any injury."

"You don't know them as I do. Desperate fellows like the Dawsons will do anything at times."

"Dashaway, don't you think you are rather hard on them—and on me?"

"I know the Dawsons—I don't know much about you."

"I am not so bad as you think I am."

"Then why don't you set me free?"

"We won't discuss that, now. You had better think it over."

"I have thought it over. I am grateful to you for saving me, but—well at present I can't do anything."

"You mean, you won't."

"Well, have it that way if you wish."

"You'll be sorry some day," said Dave, bluntly.

Ridgely left the room. He closed the door after him with an assurance to Dave that things would be "all right." Just then there was the sound of some one hurrying into the next room, and an excited voice shouted out in an exultant tone:

CHAPTER XXIII

HIRAM'S ADVENTURES

The young aviator at once recognized the voice in the adjoining room which spoke the excited, words:

"We've got the other one, too!"

It was Jerry Dawson who had spoken. Dave knew that the statement could refer to no other than his missing chum. Dave was in something of a flutter of suspense. Then his eye brightened and a cheery smile overspread his face, as he caught the words in a dearly familiar tone:

"Say, do you want to kill a fellow?"

It was Hiram who spoke, in a resentful and disgusted voice. Its accents were as pert and ringing as ever, and Dave was overjoyed to know that his loyal comrade was alive and apparently unhurt.

"Say, Dawson," here broke in Ridgely, "I want to speak to you."

"Put this fellow in with Dashaway," ordered Jerry, and then the door of Dave's prison place was pulled open. A familiar form came limping and stumbling across the threshold, and the door was slammed to and locked after him.

"Hiram!" cried Dave in genuine delight.

He drew back as his friend faced him. He had noticed that Hiram limped. Now he saw that one arm was in a sling. Besides that, Hiram's face was one mass of cuts and scratches. One eye was nearly closed.

"Oh, Hiram!" cried Dave aghast.

"Look is if I'd been through a threshing machine, do I?" grinned the plucky lad.

"What happened?" asked Dave seriously.

"Dave," declared Hiram almost solemnly, "I honestly don't know. The machine drove upwards so quickly I wondered if some jar or the broken wire that was switching about didn't start the lever. By the time I got to the pilot's seat the machine was on a terrific whiz."

"What did you do?" asked Dave.

"Not much of anything, except to get rattled," confessed Hiram. "I tried to circle, and she went banking. Then the Machine took the prettiest drift you ever saw. All of a sudden one of the planes dropped and then we landed."

"Where?"

"On top of some trees. Right beyond was a deep basin, chuck full of undergrowth. The machine just took a slide off the tops of the trees, and slipped down to the bottom of the basin. Then she turned, I was thrown out."

"What then, Hiram?" pressed Dave in a concerned way.

"Well, Dave, we had briers and brambles on the farm, but nothing to compare with those Canadian thistles, or whatever they were. Look at my face."

"And your arm?"

Hiram shrugged his shoulders resignedly.

"The half breed who looked at it said it was broken. He seemed to be some kind of an Indian doctor. He rubbed my scratches and bruises with some leaves and set my arm in splints."

"Why, where did the half breed come in?" inquired Dave.

"Well, as soon as I got my wits from the tumble, I thought of you. I tried to get up out of the basin, but the sides were so steep I couldn't make it. So I— well, Dave," added Hiram with a queer laugh, "I sort of busied myself about the airship. It wasn't much battered up. I feared the Dawson crowd might come hunting for the machine, so—well, I sort of busied myself about the airship," repeated Hiram, with a strange chuckle. "I was resting when that half breed and another fellow came along. The Indian is a great trailer, I guess, for he was sharp enough to notice the tree tops and the bushes the machine had rolled over. Anyhow, down he came on a rope into the basin and found me."

"And the Monarch II," said Dave.

"No, he didn't find the machine," declared Hiram.

"But—"

"Let me tell my story, Dave," interrupted Hiram. "He got me up aloft. Then he said I was badly hurt, and started in to mend me up. Then they brought me here. They kept talking about the airship, and tried to make me tell where it was. I wouldn't, and didn't."

"Wasn't it in the basin you spoke of?" inquired Dave wonderingly.

"Yes."

"Then why—?"

"Hush! We're going to have visitors."

This was true. There was a sound at the door of their prison room, and the padlock was displaced. Jerry Dawson stepped into view, his father behind him.

"Well," he said, with a leer meant to be clever, "I suppose you fellows know me?"

"We know you, Jerry," retorted Hiram, "only too well."

"I'm boss here," boasted Jerry.

"That's fine, isn't it?" said Hiram.

"And I've got you. We'll have your airship soon, too. You'll do some walking getting back home, I'm thinking."

"What do you want of us, Jerry?" inquired Dave, coolly.

"I want to know where that airship of yours is in the first place."

"Put it in the last place, Jerry," suggested Hiram, "for you won't find out from me."

"I'll bet I will," vaunted Jerry. "I have a good mind to punch you for making all the mischief you have."

"You're safe, Jerry, seeing I'm disabled," said Hiram.

"Bah! Say, Dashaway, who's working against us here or across the lake besides yourself?"

"You will have to, guess that, Jerry," replied Dave.

"You won't tell?"

"No. I'll say this, though: You had better try to even up things in some way. The Interstate people and the government know all about you, and you are likely to have some explaining to do."

Jerry looked worried, but he feigned indifference.

"I'll keep you two safe and quiet till I get ready to quit, all the same," he snapped out, and slammed the door shut and locked it.

Dave and Hiram listened in silence for some minutes to sounds in the next room.

They could only catch the echo of voices. Jerry and his father seemed to be engaged in conversation.

Suddenly there was an interruption. There was the sound of an excited voice, drawing nearer each moment.

A door slammed. Then heavy running footsteps echoed out, ending only as some one appeared to burst unceremoniously into the next room.

"What's the row?" the boys heard in the gruff tones of Jerry's father.

"Say!" shouted the intruder, evidently a member of their group, "they've done it!"

"Who have?" shouted out Jerry quickly.

"The revenuers."

"What do you mean?"

"They got Ridgely."

A cry of dismay and excitement ran through the next room.

"How do you know?" demanded the elder Dawson.

"I saw them myself—right near Brantford. What's more, they're coming this way to get the rest of us."

At this announcement came another cry.

"You are sure of that?"

"When was this?"

"How soon will they be here?"

"Who is responsible for this?"

So the cries and questions ran on. There was an excited discussion all around.

"Maybe Ridgely is a turncoat!" cried somebody.

"Well, we can't talk about that now—we must look out for ourselves," said another.

"Right you are. Let us get out of here as soon as we possibly can!"

"That's the talk!"

CHAPTER XXIV

THE ESCAPE BY AIRCRAFT

"That's good," instantly cried Hiram Dobbs. "They'll have troubles of their own now, maybe."

He and Dave listening closely, could now detect bustle and excitement in the rooms beyond their own prison place.

They could hear Jerry Dawson fussing and bawling about, while his father's gruff voice seemed to give orders to the men in the place.

"I wonder what they will do with us now?" inquired Hiram.

"We shall probably soon know," returned Dave.

"Get those fellows out of there, you two," they finally heard Jerry

Dawson order.

The door of the prison room was unlocked and thrown open.

"March out," ordered Jerry.

Dave and Hiram took their time about obeying the mandate. Then at a word from Jerry two of his men hastened them across the threshold, seizing them by the arms.

"Ouch!" roared Hiram. "Do you want to smash my arm all over again?"

The man who held him was less rough at this. In the room the boys saw Jerry, his father, the two men who held them and three others. Before Dawson lay a large, round bundle. A smaller one lay at the feet of one of the other men.

"Now, then," spoke Dawson, "ready and quick is the word. I've divided it up fair, and you'll find your share in that bundle. You three had better get it and yourselves to some safe place."

"Yes," spoke one of the men, "the revenuers will surely be here soon."

"You two," continued Dawson to the men had Dave and Hiram in charge, "bring the boys along."

"Where to?" was asked.

"Just follow us," was the surly response.

"Give a hand, Jerry."

The two Dawsons lifted the bundle at their feet and started from the room. There were sounds as if some one was pounding on the door at the front of the building. The Dawsons, however, did not go that way. They quickened their steps, the captives were led through several rooms, and finally a door at the rear of the place was opened.

"Hold them tight now," ordered Jerry.

"Yes, and if they make any outcry quiet them the way you know how," added his father.

Dave and Hiram were surprised to find themselves now in complete darkness.

"We're going through some kind of a tunnel," whispered the young aviator to his companion a moment later.

Their captors forced them along in the steps of the Dawsons. They must have proceeded several hundred feet thus, when the tunnel grew lighter. Then they arrived at an exit letting out into a deep, narrow ravine.

"They must have taken this route to escape from the revenue officers," Dave told his companion, in a guarded tone.

"Shall we set up a fight and yell?" proposed the audacious Hiram.

"Not with that broken arm of yours and four to one," dissented Dave.

"Broken arm, nothing! Say-hello! Why, they're taking us to their airship!" exclaimed Hiram.

They had come upon the Drifter at a point where the ravine spread out and a long level space showed.

"Now then, brisk is the word," spoke the elder Dawson.

He and his son carried the bundle up to the Drifter and managed to stow it aboard. Jerry climbed into the pilot's seat. His father drew some stout double cord from his pocket.

"Tie up those boys hand and foot," he ordered grimly.

"See here, Mr. Dawson," spoke up Dave, "what are you going to do with us?"

"You'll find that out very soon," was the gruff reply.

The two men proceeded to secure the arms and feet of the captives.

Dave knew it was useless to resist the rough treatment he received.

Hiram was not so patient.

"Say, this is an outrage!" he cried out.

"What's the matter with you?" demanded Jerry Dawson, leaning from his seat with a scowl on his face.

"What do you want to tie a one-armed fellow up for?" grumbled Hiram.

"That's so," said the elder Dawson. "Just attend to his feet and one arm. No use making him safer. He won't be very dangerous with only a broken arm free."

First Dave and then Hiram were lifted into the seats behind the pilot's post. As has been said, the Drifter could carry five passengers, and they were not crowded or uncomfortable.

"They are going to carry us away with them," whispered Hiram to his companion.

"Let them," replied the young aviator. "It may give us a chance to outwit them someplace along the line."

Hiram chuckled. Dave stared at him strangely, but his doughty companion did not explain what he had in his mind.

"All ready," announced Jerry, his hand on his lever.

His father got into the seat behind him.

"Wait a minute," he spoke to his son. "You two," he added to the men who had accompanied them, "better get to your friends, divide up your plunder and make yourselves scarce as soon as you can."

"That's what we intend to do," replied one of the men.

"Hold on!" exclaimed his companion, suddenly turning around at the echo of a loud shout.

"What's the trouble now, I wonder?"

"Hey, stop the airship! Stop them! Stop them!" yelled the strident voice of a man coming pell mell down the ravine path. He was in a frantic state of excitement and waving his arms wildly.

"Don't lose a second," spoke Dawson quickly.

Jerry gave the starter a whirl. Dave noticed that his father was quite excited and kept watching the advancing runner.

"Stop them, I tell you!" yelled this individual whom Dave recognized as one of the three individuals left behind at the hut with the other bundle.

"What for?" shouted one of the two men near the airship.

"Robbers-thieves! That bundle they gave us!"

"What about it?"

"No silks—nothing but a lot of worthless truck. They've cheated us and are making away with the real plunder."

Whiz! up went the airship. The three men ran after it. The newcomer shook his fist vengefully after the machine. The other two picked up rocks and hurled them in its wake.

"O. K.," chuckled Jerry, as the Drifter shot far out of reach of their deluded confederates.

"Do your level best, Jerry," spoke his father.

"The revenue men may have another airship in commission."

"Oh, I guess not," retorted Jerry airily. "Say, what about the one these fellows had?"

"They know and won't tell. Some of crowd will find it, though I told them if they did to dismantle it. They can get something for the old junk."

"About all they will get, eh?" leered Jerry.

"I'm thinking so."

"You didn't give them any of the silk?"

"Not I."

"That was slick," chuckled Jerry.

"Hear him! He's a fine one, isn't he?" observed Hiram to Dave.

"Yes, Jerry can't be true, even to his friends," replied the young aviator.

Dave watched Jerry at the lever. He had to admit that his enemy knew considerable about running an aircraft. The only criticism he could make was that several times Jerry took some big risks in daringly banking, when the least variation of the wind would have made the Drifter turn turtle.

It was six hours later when the airship descended. At times the machine had made fully sixty miles an hour. Long since they had passed the apparent limits of civilization. The course was due northwest. Vast forests spread out under them. It was only for the first time in one hundred miles, as they neared a small settlement on a river, that Jerry let down on the speed, and they descended at a spot about a mile from a settlement in the center of a big field.

Dave and Hiram were left in the chassis, while Jerry and his father left the machine. They conversed for some time, then it was arranged that Jerry should proceed to the settlement and purchase some provisions. His father came up to the machine as Jerry departed.

"See here, you two," he spoke in his usual gruff way, "we'll give you something to eat and, drink when Jerry comes back."

"Where are you taking us to, Mr. Dawson?" asked the young aviator.

"We are taking you so far from home, that you can't tramp back in time to pat any more of your friends on our track," was the blunt reply. "Another couple of hundred miles, and, if you behave yourself, we'll set you loose."

The man spoke as if the proposition was perfectly simple and honest one.

"Another couple of hundred miles?" repeated Dave.

"That is what I said, Dashaway."

"You are carrying things with a high hand, Mr. Dawson."

"Yes? Well, I know what I am doing."

"You may overreach yourself."

"Humph! I'll take my chances on that. You are smart, Dashaway, but you can't scare me and you can't get the best of me."

"But the law will get you, some day or another."

"Bah! I'm tired and don't want to listen to your talk. I tell you I know what I am doing."

"You won't release us now?"

"No."

"That is final?"

"It certainly is, and you may as well save your breath and not mention it again. I am tired out and don't want any more of such talk."

"Well, see here—" broke in Hiram.

"I won't listen to any more. Shut up."

With the words Dawson went over to a hammock at a little distance, spread his coat over it, and lay down to rest. It was not five minutes before his captives could hear him snoring loudly.

Hiram had been watching his every movement in an intense way. Now he leaned over towards Dave. His eyes were snapping with excitement and there was a broad smile on his face, as he whispered into the ear of the young aviator one word. It was:

"Hurrah!"

CHAPTER XXV

CAUGHT CONCLUSION

"Hurrah!" was the word that Hiram Dobbs spoke exultantly, and Dave looked at him in profound surprise.

Hiram had lifted himself up from the seat. Now he went through some movements that almost startled the puzzled young aviator.

Suddenly his arm shot out of the sling, and as suddenly Hiram, though with a wince, swung it around once or twice, and the three splints holding it cracked and split audibly.

"Hey, Hiram!" gasped Dave.

"S-sh!" uttered his assistant warningly.

Hiram ran his free hand down into his pocket. He drew out the big pocket knife he carried. It was more of a tool than a whittling toy, for he used it in tinkering about the airship.

With his teeth, Hiram opened its largest blade. He gave a slash at the cords surrounding his other arm and his feet. Then he leaned over towards Dave. A few deft strokes of the keen blade, and Dave, like himself, was free.

"Easy," he whispered, as Dave started up. "I'll watch Dawson. You get into the pilot's seat."

"Good for you, Hiram!" whispered back the young aviator, fairly thrilling with the excitement of the moment.

Dave took in every detail of the mechanism before his eyes. He made sure of no faulty start.

"All ready," he announced after a minute or two.

"Good-bye!" spoke Hiram, with a gay bold wave of his hand in the direction of the sleeping, Dawson.

"Put on the muffler," ordered Dave, as the exhaust began to sizzle.

Hiram did so. It was too late, however, to avoid sounding a warning to Dawson. The big man started up with a yell. He came to his feet roaring out:

"Come back!"

"I hope you'll find the walking good!" shouted Hiram, waving his hand in adieu to the amazed Dawson.

"Hiram, you're a genius!" cried Dave.

The Drifter struck a course as true as a die. The splendid machine and the young aviator were both at their best. There was a last fading picture of a forlorn man convulsed with rage and despair. Then the two boy aeronauts turned their back on the enemies who had been hoisted by their own petard.

"It's great, its grand," cheered Hiram, bubbling over with joy, as the exhilarating air and their magical progress made him realize what freedom meant to its fullest extent.

"I don't understand. Your arm, Hiram?" said Dave.

His jolly assistant waved the arm in question gaily.

"Wasn't it hurt?"

"Yes, and badly, I thought," reflected Hiram. "It was numb and useless when the half breed attended to it, but he was mistaken and so was I in thinking that any bones were broken."

"They were not?"

"Not a bit of it. Don't you see? It pains, and I'm bragging when I swing it around as if it was as good as ever, but I can use it."

"You have used it to a grand purpose, Hiram."

"I didn't notice that I could use it until they locked me up with you."

"Why didn't you tell me then?"

"Oh, I wanted to surprise you."

"You have, Hiram."

"I thought I'd play 'possum on those smart fellows. I played the cripple strong. You see what has come of it."

When they had gone nearly one hundred miles, Dave saw that the gasoline supply was running low. Luckily they were near a little town. They made a descent on a river, much to the delight and wonder of the whole place, bought a new supply, and resumed their flight.

It was after ten o'clock in the evening when the welcome lights of Anseton came into view. Dave did not look around for some hiding place on the outskirts on this occasion. He startled a drowsy policeman by landing in the middle of some vacant lots on his beat.

A brief explanation was made to the officer, and a man hired to watch the Drifter until they returned. Then Dave and Hiram hurried to the hotel in Anseton where Mr. Price made his headquarters.

The revenue officer was found. He listened to the story of the two young aviators in amazement and admiration. Then he reported results of his own efforts.

Ridgely was under arrest, two of his accomplices were being then pursued by his assistants, and the smuggling combination was all broken up.

"The clews you have given us were fine ones, Dashaway," said the official gratefully. "You have done the government a vast service, I can tell you."

Mr. Price insisted on the boys taking a needed rest. He sent one of his men to guard the Drifter, and, after a famous meal, made his guests agree to sleep in a comfortable bed for the first time in nearly a week.

It was just after they had entered their room that Dave made the remark.

"You know we had better see if those friends of the Dawsons have found the Monarch II and made away with it, Hiram."

"Well, I can tell you that they haven't," replied Hiram, with a confident chuckle.

"How can you know that?"

"Why, Dave, when I was shut in with the machine in that basin, I took it apart. You know it was made to do that, so it could be shipped readily. Well, I'll bet you I hid those parts in places in that basin where nobody can locate them but myself."

"Good for you!" commended Dave heartily.

"I think the Interstate people will have something pleasant to say to you when they know all the wonders you've done in chasing their stolen airship."

It was the brightest day in the year, it seemed to the two young aviators, as they reached Columbus by train, and started at once for Mr. King's hangar.

Old Grimshaw had met them at the depot. He was full of friendly chatter, seemed to be chuckling over some secret surprise he had in store for them, and rushed them towards the headquarters of the Aegis.

"Yes, Mr. King is back," he advised the boys.

"Did he find Mr. Dale?" inquired Dave anxiously.

"He'll tell you."

Dave and Hiram had much to relate. Two boys probably never received a more pleasant welcome than they, when with the Drifter they reported to the manager of the Interstate Aeroplane Company.

Mr. Randolph had the president and two directors of the concern on hand to meet them. Their stirring story was taken in by the august business men with an attention and appreciation that of itself paid the lads well for all the duty done.

The boys had remained long enough at Anseton to have some men go with them and locate the hidden sections of the Monarch II, and arrange to have them shipped by rail back to the factory.

Dave felt pretty rich when he left the Interstate works with a check for five hundred dollars in his pocket, and an offer of advanced employment for himself and his loyal and useful assistant for two seasons ahead.

"I want to see Mr. King before I decide what I will do," Dave told Mr. Randolph, his mind full of the much discussed flight across the Atlantic in the giant airship. "You can have your two hundred and fifty dollars any time you like, Hiram." he added to his chum on their way to the depot.

As they now reached the Aegis hangar, Grimshaw stepped aside with a pleased laugh.

"Safe and sound and famous. Here they are, Mr. King!" he shouted.

"There's no doubt of that," chorused the friendly voice of the expert aviator. "Dave! Hiram! A thousand times welcome."

If he had been own father to the lads, Mr. King could not have greeted them more affectionately.

"You've done us all proud, Dashaway," he declared. "Got a telegram from the Interstate folks, and the noon paper. The paper has given you two columns. This way. A friend waiting to see you."

Mr. King pushed Dave across the little room in the hangar he used as an office.

A middle aged, noble looking gentleman arose from a chair as Dave entered. His face was beaming, and there was an eager light in his eyes.

"Dave Dashaway?" he said, half inquiringly.

"Yes, sir," assented Dave, grasping the extended hand of the gentleman.

"My best and oldest friend's boy," continued the gentleman.

"It is Mr. Dale, Dashaway," spoke Mr. King, following Dave into the room.

Somehow the young aviator felt his heart warm to the man of whom he had heard so much, but had never before seen. The old gentleman's eyes rested on him in a kindly earnest way that made Dave feel less lonely in the world.

Briefly Mr. King told of the chase he had made to locate Mr. Dale.

"I've got a long story to tell," said the aviator, when he could get a chance to talk. He turned to Mr. Dale. "That is, if you wish me to tell it," he added.

"Certainly," was the ready reply. "You can probably tell it better than I can."

"Well, to begin with, it was no easy task to get on the track of this fellow Gregg," commenced the well-known aviator. "I had to do some tall hunting before I could locate him and his two cronies."

"His cronies?" repeated Dave.

"Yes, he had two fellows in the game with him. I guess he found out that he could not manage it alone. The three of them called on Mr. Dale and at first got him to take an automobile ride. Then they took him to a lonely house down near Slaytown, and there they kept him a prisoner."

"A prisoner!"

"Yes."

"Just as we were kept prisoners," muttered our hero.

"Mr. Dale says he was treated very nicely, for Gregg no doubt, had an idea he could get more money that way."

"Well, after a good deal of hard work I located the spot and saw Mr. Dale from a distance. I knew I could not rescue him single handed, so I went back to town and notified the police. I had hard work getting three officers to accompany me, because the police just then were having their annual inspection and parade and all wanted to be present. When we got to the lonely house we got a big surprise."

"How was that?"

"Gregg and the two men and Mr. Dale were gone."

"Where to?"

"At first I couldn't find out. But we saw wagon tracks in the soft roadbed and followed these along the road and through a big field. Presently we came to a patch of woods, and there found what in years gone by had been a lumber camp. At the old house we saw a horse and wagon, and we knew the crowd must be somewhere around. We separated, and came up to the place from all sides. In a shed near the house we found Gregg and the two men. They were discussing the situation, when we pounced on them and surprised them."

"Did they resist?"

"Gregg did, and as a consequence he got a blow in the mouth from a policeman's club that broke off two of his teeth. Then all of the crowd gave up, and we handcuffed the lot and made them prisoners."

"And Mr. Dale?" asked Dave, with interest.

"We found him in the old house, tied up."

"And very grateful for the rescue," put in the old gentleman, warmly.

"All of us came to town in the wagon the rascals had hired. Then Gregg and his accomplices were put in jail, and Mr. Dale and I came on here," concluded Mr. King.

"I am mighty happy to see things have turned out this way," said our hero, heartily.

"I am so glad to find the son of my old balloonist friend," said Mr. Dale, "that I shall have to adopt you legally, Dave, before you slip away from me again. Let me be your second father, my boy, and take an interest in your progress. I stayed over here with our mutual friend, Mr. King, purposely to go over this wonderful plan to cross the Atlantic in an airship."

"Then you think well of it?" asked Dave.

"You do not have to ask that of an old aeronaut enthusiast, my boy," replied Mr. Dale.

"Yes, Dashaway," said the aviator, "Mr. Dale has promised gladly to furnish the capital to put through our newest giant airship scheme."

So, for the present, we leave Dave Dashaway, the young aviator, and his friends. What happened to them in their new and daring project, will be told in the next volume of this series, to be called, "Dave Dashaway and His Giant Airship; Or, A Marvelous Trip Across the Atlantic."

The young aviator had won his way through pluck and perseverance. Dave had already done some great things in his apprenticeship as a junior aeronaut.

Now, the friend, and assistant of a noted expert in aeronautics, he was eager and buoyant at the prospect of winning fame and fortune in an attempt that was the dream of the expert airman of the world.

THE END

9 781836 573692